Secrets at St Jude's

Also by Carmen Reid,
for adult readers:

The Personal Shopper
Did the Earth Move?
Three in a Bed
Up All Night
How Was it For You?

Secrets at St Jude's

New Girl

CORGI BOOKS

SECRETS AT ST JUDE'S: NEW GIRL
A CORGI BOOK 978 0 552 55706 1

Published in Great Britain by Corgi Books,
an imprint of Random House Children's Books
A Random House Group Company

This edition published 2008

3 5 7 9 10 8 6 4

The Random House Group Limited supports the Forest Stewardship Council
(FSC), the leading international forest certification organization. All our titles
that are printed on Greenpeace-approved FSC-certified paper carry the FSC
logo. Our paper procurement policy can be found at
www.rbooks.co.uk/environment.

Mixed Sources
Product group from well-managed
forests and other controlled sources
www.fsc.org Cert no. TT-COC-2139
© 1996 Forest Stewardship Council

Set in 12/16pt Minion by
Falcon Oast Graphic Art Ltd.

Corgi Books are published by Random House Children's Books,
61–63 Uxbridge Road, London W5 5SA

www.**kids**at**randomhouse**.co.uk
www.**rbooks**.co.uk

Addresses for companies within The Random House Group Limited
can be found at: www.randomhouse.co.uk/offices.htm

THE RANDOM HOUSE GROUP Limited Reg. No. 954009

A CIP catalogue record for this book is available from the British Library.

Printed in the UK by CPI Bookmarque, Croydon, CR0 4TD

Chapter One

Gina Peterson didn't hear the electric ~~gates~~ car slide open, or the silver Mercedes convertible purr through into the drive. She didn't hear the heavy wrought-iron and glass front door slam shut, or the *tappity-tap* of her mother's elegant high heels on the parquet floor of the huge, jaw-droppingly impressive entrance hall.

Over the noise in her bedroom, Gina had no hope of hearing her mother's screech of fury as she took the white marble-topped stairs at something as close to a run as she could manage, what with the heels and the fact that she was pulling a tired eight-year-old boy along behind her.

'*Gina!*' Lorelei Winkelmann screamed at the top of her voice, furious that, yet again, she was going to have a row with her spoiled brat of a daughter.

It was almost 7 p.m. (Pacific Time) and something of an all-girl party was going on in Gina's rooms: her

1

three best friends, Paula, Ria and Maddison, had come over to the house after school.

House wasn't quite the right word for the place. The Winkelmann, Royce and Peterson family home in Malibu, California, was one of those stunning glass modernist fantasies with enormous windows, billowing curtains and a sparkling view of endless ocean and sky.

The bright turquoise swimming pool in the garden was long enough for Lorelei's fifty laps at 6.20 a.m. to be properly invigorating. Naturally, there was a gardener who mowed the lawns, trimmed the shrubbery and watered the plants all day long, while indoors a housekeeper buffed the maple, chrome and marble surfaces to dazzling perfection.

Gina and her half-brother, Menzie Royce, had lived in this luxury for as long as they could both remember, with not just a room of their own, but a whole suite – bedroom, sitting room and personalized bathroom (Gina's was pink with gold taps; Menzie had recently chosen an elaborate Superman mosaic for his shower, which he was already acutely embarrassed about).

Whenever people asked Gina what Lorelei and her partner, Mick, Menzie's dad, did for a living, Gina's glib reply was: 'Oh, computers . . . software, you know, that kind of stuff. They practically invented the Internet.'

Maddison and Ria were sprawled across Gina's double bed, taking turns to paint each other's finger-nails in the moment's shade of 'Screaming Queen' pink, while Paula and Gina were practising their dance moves to the retro-disco belting out from the surround-sound stereo. All four were decked out in 'awesome' (or, to the uninitiated, 'ludicrous') new outfits chosen at great length from the landslide of expensive tops, skirts, jeans, shoes, bags, jewellery, jackets and sunglasses spread across the floor, the bed, the sofa and as far as the eye could see.

'Man, we rock!' Gina panted, gyrating her hips in time with Paula's and attempting a complicated move that was more painful than she'd expected in the shoes she'd borrowed from her mother's wardrobe. 'I can't wait for next weekend! I. Can. Not. Wait.'

'So has your mom OK'd everything?' Paula asked loudly, so as to be heard over the music.

'Oh . . . you know . . . I'll tell her you're going and your mom's said it's OK, so that will be' – Gina put her hands behind her head, flicked up her long blonde hair and carried on dancing as best she could in three-inch heels – 'cool.'

She, Paula, Ria and Maddison had a plan. The weekend after next they were going to hook up with Paula's boyfriend, Martinez, and three of his friends, including Aidan. Yes, most definitely including Aidan. Gina got that stupid, trippy, butterfly-stomach feeling whenever she thought about Aidan, but that didn't stop her worrying a lot about whether he liked Ria better than her. Gina imagined going for long walks with Aidan, talking to him, holding his hand and feeling his arm around her shoulders. But she didn't like to think about kissing him. Because just *thinking* about kissing brought on flashbacks of her last boyfriend: Squid Boy, so named because he had turned out to be damp, slimy, squelchy and tentacle-armed. Gina shuddered and tried to put the Squid out of her mind.

Anyway, the eight of them were all going to take a bus up-state to the Water's Edge Festival to see some of the coolest, most happening bands in the world, and they were going to camp for two nights in adjoining tents. Paula and Martinez had already organized the tents; had in fact taken quite a close interest in the sleeping arrangements.

'You can't lose your virginity in a tent you're sharing with your friends,' Gina had warned. 'It's just not romantic . . . or polite.'

'As if!' Paula had hissed back.

The trip was organized, the tents and sleeping bags had been bought, the festival tickets booked. There were just a few tiny details to tie up . . . like, mmmmm, getting their parents to agree. Everyone had been so scared their parents would say no that no one seemed to have actually asked yet.

'I was going to tell my mom that your mom had already agreed,' Paula said, breaking into the kind of groovy little on-the-spot moonwalk that proved, yet again, she was the best dancer.

Gina had been dancing with Paula and copying her every move since first grade, but it didn't make any difference: Paula was a natural and Gina was the kind of dancer who twisted her ankles.

'Not a problem,' Gina told Paula now. 'Our moms are far too busy to actually speak to each other. Jeez, they're both such classic over-achievers.' She glanced down at her little silver wristwatch, which was Gucci (of course), just as most of her tops were Juicy and her jeans 7 For All Mankind. In Gina's group these were the current shopping rules, which had to be obeyed.

'It's only seven,' Gina added. 'Mine won't be home for at least another hour, or later if she's doing "me time" at Power Pilates. Yours?'

'Same,' Paula replied.

So all four girls were a little surprised, to say the least, when the bedroom door burst open and they saw Gina's mother, Lorelei, towering before them, all heels, piled-up hair and slick skirt suit, shouting at the top of her voice: '*What are you doing?! What the hell is going on in here?!*'

'Hey, get back in your box, Mom,' was Gina's amazingly cool response. Much as she was used to these regular rants, she did at least have the sense to pick up the remote and snap off the music.

In the sudden silence, Paula, Ria and Maddison stood rooted to the spot, although one glance at Ms Winkelmann's face told them they needed to pack up and get out of there just as quickly as their legs could carry them.

'Look at this place!' Lorelei began, surveying the nuclear damage that four girls in search of the perfect outfit can inflict on a teenage bedroom. 'Look at *you*! You look totally ridiculous!' she added, taking in Gina's crop top, emblazoned with the logo RICH & SKINNY, the denim miniskirt, purple and blue striped leg warmers and then, catastrophically, Lorelei's own very new black patent-leather T-bar heels.

'My shoes!' she shrieked. 'Take them off at once.'

6

'All right.' Gina glared back, daring to meet her mother eye to eye and folding her arms defiantly across her (still, despite all those exercises, 32 B) chest.

'Don't you dare look at me like that!' Lorelei stormed. 'I want an explanation and I want a really big apology or you don't get one cent in allowance for a very long time.'

'What for?' came Gina's outraged response as her friends began to quietly gather up their things and sidle towards the door.

'Oh, you've forgotten who this is, have you?' Lorelei pulled her left hand forward and Menzie stepped out from behind her legs.

For a moment Gina didn't answer. She was doing the math. Was today Friday, by any chance? Because on Fridays she was supposed to get a cab from her school and go straight to Menzie's school to collect him. Then she was supposed to bring him home and look after him until Lorelei or Mick's return.

Because she had forgotten to show up at Menzie's school several times before, Lorelei always called her on her cell phone to remind her, but then Gina had left her cell in her locker, hadn't she?

And the home landline had been busy all afternoon because Ria had been on it for hours trying to book an extra Water's Edge ticket. And Lorelei wouldn't have been able to call Dominique, their housekeeper, because today was her day off. And even if Lorelei had managed to get hold of a neighbour, Gina wouldn't have heard the front doorbell because the music was so loud.

So – to conclude – Lorelei must have had to leave her very, very important meeting or whatever it was she was doing that afternoon, speed down the highway to Menzie's school and finally pick him up from the janitor, or wherever he'd been for the past two hours, and bring him home herself – which might explain why she was so eye-poppingly, outrageously furious.

Ooops.

'I think I'll head off now, Ms Winkelmann,' said Paula, edging past Lorelei and out of the door.

Lorelei glared at Paula, held out her hand and snapped, 'My necklace, please.' Paula obliged word-lessly.

'Yeah ... um ... got to go,' Maddison added, making her break for freedom.

'Earrings!' Lorelei commanded. Maddison un-clipped the pearls and surrendered them.

Ria followed on quickly, handing over a fringed silk scarf and mumbling something nervous-sounding.

'I'm sorry, Mom. Jeez . . . I'm really sorry, Menzie,' Gina said as contritely as she could.

But the bedroom door just slammed shut and she was left alone in her mother's shoes and the stupid legwarmers with a mountain of stuff to put away.

Gina picked up the remote and switched the music back on, then flung herself down on the bed. The worst thing was she'd have to wait absolutely hours now before she could ask her mother about going to the festival.

'And turn that garbage off!' came a shout from the other side of the door.

It was close to 10 p.m. when Gina dared to leave her room in search of her family again. When she'd come down an hour earlier, she'd found a chicken salad set out for her in the kitchen, but it was obvious her mother and Menzie had already eaten and were now busy with Menzie's bedtime. Unfortunately Mick, a welcome and soothing influence on her mom, wasn't home yet. Gina had bolted down the salad and headed back to her room.

Now, as she came down the stairs, she saw the light was on in her mom's home office; she could hear the

TV at low volume. She opened the door quietly and tiptoed in.

Lorelei was at her desk, staring with concentration at the big computer screen in front of her. Her dark blonde hair had begun to slide out of the tight up-do she kept it in for work, but she was still in her silk blouse and skirt. As flip-flops had replaced the heels and there was a glass of white wine crammed full of ice on her desk, Gina knew that her mother was winding down for the evening.

'Mommy?' she said, approaching the desk. 'I'm really sorry about Menzie. I'm really sorry you had to come and get him. I won't forget again. I promise.'

Lorelei turned from the computer screen and gave just the tiniest of half-smiles in Gina's direction.

'Gina,' she said quietly. 'Gina, Gina, Gina . . . What am I going to do with you? What am I going to do?'

Gina decided it was safe to get a little closer, so she put her hands on her mother's shoulders and began to rub at the tight muscles a little.

'I'm still really annoyed with you – there's no use trying to butter me up,' Lorelei began. 'And I might as well tell you straight off that I know about the festival, and Paula's mother and I are in agreement. No way. Definitely not.'

Gina's attempt at a massage stopped abruptly at this news.

'What?!' came the outraged voice Lorelei knew so well.

'Really, Gina.' Her mother turned to face her. 'Did you seriously think I was going to let you go off with some guys I've never met to who knows where, doing who knows what, when it's not even the holidays and I know you're way behind with your schoolwork and your grades are slipping?'

Gina felt a surge of anger sweep through her as she thought of the trip: of the two tents and four boys, of her sleeping bag, which was bright red, of her ticket, stored safely in her jewellery box upstairs, and of Aidan and the fact that now Ria would be at the festival with him and not her . . .

'I want to go!' she yelled. 'I *have* to go! There is no way that I can't go!'

'You're so spoiled, Gina!' her mother replied in a tone that was rising rapidly. 'You have no idea how lucky you are, how much freedom you already have . . . and how much stuff!' she added. 'When I was a teenager . . .'

Good grief, Gina so didn't want to hear this; she rolled her eyes theatrically. Her mother had never been a teenager! Well, obviously she had, but everything Lorelei had ever told her about *her* teenage years proved to Gina that she was the daughter of a total geek.

Her mother had been a robot teen: the kind who does extra homework for fun, gets amazing grades, becomes captain of the school debating team, never even notices a single boy.

Gina's mother had been the cleverest girl in her year; Gina's mother had gone to a top university; Gina's mother had won trophies for 'outstanding achievement'; Gina's mother had been presented to the Queen of England; Gina's mother had a lump on her middle finger from writing so many hundreds of pages of notes and essays when she was a teenager – '*We didn't have computers then, you know.*'

In short, Gina's mother was perfect and Gina didn't have a hope of ever living up to her. So why bother even trying?

'You can't go,' her mother said firmly. 'You can't go because, guess what? You won't be here,' she added.

'What?!' What was her mother talking about now?

'I've had enough of this,' Lorelei said sharply. 'I'm exhausted with you. I'm exhausted with fighting all the time, picking up after you, sorting out your messes, solving your problems, doing your homework, Gina! I've just looked through the maths project you're intending to hand in and it's all wrong. Needs total re-working.'

Gina managed to gasp out an exasperated 'But . . . !' as she was handed her homework folder, which had been taken from her school bag without her permission, before Lorelei stormed on.

'I no longer want to watch you change from an A student into a D, maybe even an F if you keep at it. I'm about to take on a really important new project. I'm going to be working all the time. It's a great, *great* opportunity! So I've hired a nanny to look after Menzie out of school . . . But for you, Gina, for you we really need to do something different. We need to turn things around for you or you're going to be in trouble. All you care about is clothes, boys and being cool. No good will come of this. No good at all!'

The way Lorelei was looking at her was making Gina nervous. It sounded like she had a plan. Gina couldn't remember the last time she'd liked one of her mother's plans.

'You know about St Jude's, don't you?' Lorelei was asking her.

See, although it was hard to recognize these days, Gina's mother wasn't Californian. Or even American. She was British. No, actually her dad was German, but anyway, she had spent most of her schooldays in *Edinborrow*, or whatever it was called – some city in Scotland. Anyway, Lorelei had been sent there to some school for girls called St Jude's.

It explained a lot, Gina was sure.

'Yeah?' She crossed her arms, wondering what on earth her mother's school had to do with anything.

'I've been speaking to the headmistress of St Jude's,' Lorelei continued. 'I've told her all about you and she's very interested . . . very sympathetic.'

'Huh?' was Gina's bewildered response.

'And they have a space in the boardinghouse. Most of the pupils are in Edinburgh and go home after school, but about one hundred or so are boarders.'

'*Huh?!*' Pennies were dropping for Gina. Warning lights were clicking on and flashing up. Big time.

'Yes, you're going to start this summer semester – although it's called "term" over there – at St Jude's, in Edinburgh, in Scotland.'

'I am not!' Gina exclaimed.

But Lorelei was carrying on in her *I haven't heard you* way. 'Yup. You're going to St Jude's and you aren't coming back until you have good grades. Really good grades, Gina. I don't care how long that takes, by the way: a term, a whole year, even the rest of your school career.'

'I'm not going. No way!'

'Oh yes, you are going. The ticket's already booked. You arrive in Edinburgh on the twenty-fourth of April, the day before term starts, just like all the other boarders.'

'NO!!!'

Chapter Two

The big black taxi, which had rattled Gina about in the back seat all the way from the airport, pulled into a side street, slowed as the driver checked out the house numbers, then came to a sudden standstill. 'Number nine?' the driver asked.

'Yes . . . well . . . I think so . . . This is Bute Gardens?' she asked.

'Aye.'

She looked out of the window at the solid stone house beyond the thick pillars and bushy green hedge they'd pulled alongside. It was still raining. It had been raining since she stepped off the plane at *Edinborrow*. (It was spelled Edinburgh, by the way, but no one in Edinburgh said it like that. They said 'Edinburra'.)

Gina had been travelling for sixteen hours. For much of that time she had read, re-read and pored over the ten-page St Jude's handbook, trying desperately to imagine what this was going to be like. She had begun to picture a school full of beautiful, intelligent British girls: teenage Kates with long blonde hair and really posh voices. And at some point mid-Atlantic, she had started to convince herself that it might not be so bad: it might even be fun. In fact, maybe it would be really glamorous! Some of her classmates might even be related to Prince William . . . or at least know him!

Gina had also closely studied the photographs of the wood-panelled library, the grassy tennis courts and the soaring assembly hall, which came complete with those churchy lead-paned windows and wooden beams. It was all so old, so traditional – so positively *historical*.

'You'll make the most amazing friends,' Lorelei had promised her. 'Won't that be great? I mean, I know you love Paula, Ria and Maddison, but you've known them for ever. Wouldn't you like to meet some new people? And boarding-school friends are different,' she had gone on; 'boarding-school friends are like family.'

The taxi driver sat still. Gina sat still. Surely he wasn't expecting her to carry her bags out by herself? Jeez, what kind of service was this?

She looked in her purse and brought out the sheaf of curly notes the fare required, and because she was Californian and proud of it, she figured in a big tip as well, even though the driver was the rudest man on the planet; then she got out of the cab and hauled her two heavy black bags behind her towards the front door of number 9 Bute Gardens.

The driveway beyond the pillars was crammed full of cars, girls, luggage and parents. At the sight of so many strangers, all so different looking, Gina felt her stomach knot up. The last time she'd been a new girl at school, without a single friend, she'd been going to kindergarten for the first time and she'd had Mommy's hand to cling onto for the whole morning.

Ever since then, she'd moved up through Junior School, then Junior High, with a gang of ready-made allies.

This was new. This was *very* new, and despite all Lorelei's encouraging words, still ringing in her ears from the call made by cell phone in the back of the cab, Gina felt nervous enough to puke.

Just one look at the other girls in the driveway was enough to tell her that, despite her handbook-inspired fantasies, she was not going to fit in here. Gina was wearing heels, they were wearing sneakers; her jeans were designer, theirs were scruffy; her top and jacket were D&G, the girl in front of her was in some sort of mountaineering polar fleece. No one in a polar fleece was likely to know Prince William, were they?

The only thing that stopped Gina from calling her mom straight back to say, 'OK, big joke over, can I come home now?' was that, for once, she wanted to prove her mother wrong.

That night when Lorelei had first suggested St Jude's and Gina had been utterly horrified, her mother had thrown down the challenge: *Oh, I knew you wouldn't go, you're too scared. Too boring. Any one of your friends would have jumped at a chance like this. But not you. Eek, eek* (Lorelei had added a frightened mouse squeak for effect). *You won't even go to the mall without two of your friends holding your hands.*

Gina had listened stony-faced before declaring, 'OK then, I'll go. But only for the summer term. Just one term. I'll work hard – what else will there be to do? And then you'll let me come home again. OK?'

'It's a deal,' her mother had promised.

But now, as Gina followed the two lanky girls in the chainstore jeans up the stone steps and manhandled her bags in through the front door, boy, did she regret her decision. This was going to be awful. Forget blonde Kates, this was going to be a term in geek hell.

She stepped into a lurid hall with a red plastic floor, red and gold striped wallpaper and lots of other people who all seemed to know each other. All around her girls were kissing, hugging and shrieking greetings:

'*Suze! How are you?*'

'*Good hols? You are so brown!*'

'*Holly! Your hair! It's amazing!*'

Gina looked at her bags as if she hoped for a moment they might spring to life and start talking to her, so that she didn't feel quite so lost and awkward in this hallway.

Then a great booming female baritone broke over her. 'Aha, I spy a new girl . . . Give me one guess,' the voice exclaimed. 'Gina Winkelmann-Peterson? All the way from California? Am I right?'

Gina turned to see a smartly dressed middle-aged woman with a terrifying blonde hairdo marching over towards her.

The woman was short, but made up for this with ramrod posture and a chin that stuck high into the air. Her generously plump figure had been neatly parcelled into a plum tweed jacket and skirt enhanced with the extravagant, silky pussycat bow of a pink blouse. The hair, solid as a helmet, moved not one millimetre as the woman approached.

'Goodness me, you do look awfully tired,' the hairdo pronounced loudly, extending a hand. 'I'm Norah Knebworth, but that's Mrs Knebworth to you, the mistress of this house; your keeper, so to speak.' She squeezed Gina's hand briefly.

'Hi,' Gina said. 'Yeah, I'm Gina and I've been on a plane for, like, days.'

'Wonderful,' said Mrs Knebworth enthusiastically but inappropriately because her eye had already travelled beyond Gina's shoulder and towards the next set of parents entering through the front door. Her freshly rearranged broad and welcoming smile was now directed at them.

'Where do I go?' Gina asked, worried she was about to be left in the hall on her own again.

'Oh!' Mrs Knebworth scanned the room, then clapped a hand on the shoulder of one of the lanky, scruffy-jeaned girls and asked, 'Morag? Can you take our new girl, Gina – from California, no less – up to the Daffodil dorm?'

Morag didn't seem overjoyed at the task. She and Gina looked each other up and down. To Morag, Gina looked like an off-duty pop princess. To Gina, Morag looked like a stable girl. There just wasn't any hope that they were going to have anything in common. Why bother trying? Was every girl here going to be like this? Gina wondered.

With a shrug of her shoulders, Morag said, 'Follow me.'

Gina grasped her bags and began to haul them down a long corridor and then up a flight of carpeted wooden stairs. Then came more stairs, and even more – narrower, twisting up to the top floor.

She was struggling with the bags while Morag leaped on ahead like a damn mountain goat.

It wasn't what she wanted to do at all, but finally Gina had to say, 'Please can you help me with one of these?'

Morag wordlessly bounded back down the stairs, took hold of a bag and was now following behind Gina.

'Keep going up. It's the third floor, the attic rooms,' Morag instructed. 'First on the right.'

Finally Gina was standing in front of a slightly battered-looking white door decorated with a painted tile: a daffodil, obviously.

She waited for Morag to come up behind her, and the pause was just long enough for them both to hear:

'A new girl?!' ring out from behind the door, followed by: 'The Neb has lumped the three of us with a bloody new girl? From the States? God, I hate that woman. I absolutely *hate* her. The complete cow!'

Although Gina would have liked to wait a moment so that it wasn't quite so obvious she'd heard this, Morag pushed open the door and dumped one of the heavy black bags on the floor with the words: 'And here she is – your new girl. Hello, and welcome back to hell.'

Standing in the uncomfortable silence, all Gina could think was: *Oh, great!*

Then she cast her eyes about the room and tried to take in as much as she could. First of all she looked at the three faces turned in her direction: there was a pretty Asian girl with elbow-length black hair and molten chocolate eyes, who was wearing a sparkling pink and gold sari – though there were jeans and a geeky sweatshirt laid out on her bed as if she was about to get changed.

Sprawled across another of the narrow beds was a tall, strangely horsy-looking girl with a long, pale face, bright blue eyes and a big nose. Her jeans were grubby and tattered, and as for her jumper . . . ! Even from her position in the doorway, Gina could see the holes in the sleeves and the white dog hairs scattered across the front.

Finally Gina's eyes fell on the sophisticate of the group: a glossy, smooth and straightened blonde with red lipstick, eyeliner and base who was – halleluiah! – in the kind of hot jeans and top that Gina might have picked out for herself.

However, this good-looking, tanned girl wasn't giving off any sort of friendly vibe; in fact her look was cold and even slightly competitive. Gina understood: this girl was doing what she was doing. They were both sizing each other up and deciding which of them was prettier.

When the eye contact was over, Gina saw beyond the girls a cramped room, filled to the brim with four beds, four chests of drawers and all manner of clothes, books, tennis rackets, cases and just stuff, everywhere. Despite wall-to-wall alarmingly loud yellow and orange wallpaper, the room seemed dark and dingy. Just two small arched windows on one side let in the damp, grey evening light.

She hated it. She hated them. She hated this. Gripping her bags tightly, she wished more than anything that she could turn round, run out of this awful place and fly straight home. She'd never, ever do anything to annoy her mother ever again, never.

Then the girl with the big nose gave something of a smile, sat up on her bed, crossing her long legs underneath her, and waved Gina into the room.

'Oh, it's OK, we won't bite,' she said – in a beautiful voice, Gina couldn't help noticing. It was low and slightly husky, totally upper-class English, but so melodious. 'I'm sorry you heard what you heard. It's just that the three of us have known each other for ever. We weren't really wanting to share with anyone else.'

'Oh,' was the best Gina could offer, followed by, 'I don't really want to share with *you*.'

'Well . . . at least that's honest. This is Min, by the way' – Big Nose pointed to the Asian girl, who gave a slight smile – 'our superbabe, Amy' – this was directed at the sophisticate, who just twitched an eyebrow – 'and I'm Niffy.'

'Niffy?' Gina repeated.

'Her real name's Luella and she's always said it stinks,' Min explained.

'So, you must be Gina, the Yank?' Niffy asked.

'Yes,' Gina replied simply. *The Yank?!* She decided on the spot that if they weren't going to be friendly, then neither was she. She didn't need these dorky girls. She would just keep her head down and try and get out of this terrible place as soon as possible.

Chapter Three

'That's your bed over there, by the way. And your chest of drawers,' instructed the girl who went by the ridiculous name of Niffy.

She pointed to a narrow iron bed covered with a pink towelling bedspread. When Gina pulled the bed-spread back, she saw pink woollen blankets and white sheets pulled criminally tight round a thin mattress.

'If you fly to school, you can't bring a duvet, so you get blankets. It's grim.' This came from Min, who gestured at her similarly made-up bed. She had an unexpected accent; it took Gina a moment or two to place it: South African, maybe? A South African Asian girl?

'Just buy yourself a duvet, Min! I can't believe you've been coming here for two years and you still haven't bought yourself a duvet! They're cheap as chips.' Amy's voice was unmistakably Scottish. 'I'll buy you one. Meet me in Debenhams at the weekend.'

'OK, Miss Moneybags!' Niffy teased. 'We don't all have your dad paying our allowance every month!'

'Your dad still too busy trying to keep the leaky ancestral roof above his head, is he?' Amy shot back.

'What I want to know,' Niffy went on, ignoring the dig, 'is why Gina's been sent to us all the way from California?' She cupped her face in her hands and looked ready to listen. 'Boy trouble?' she prompted. 'Not doing well at school? Pushy mother? Or all of the above?'

'Well . . . ummm . . .' Gina was not ready to give anything away. She pulled her bags to a standstill in front of the rickety little chest of drawers and wondered how on earth she was going to fit everything she'd brought with her into this old-fashioned bit of junk. One of the drawers was half open and inside she saw several items, brand new, still in their wrappers.

She pulled out the first one: a folded cardigan, the most revolting shade of sludge green. Then came a white shirt and a grey skirt. There were socks in there too – green, scratchy woollen socks – and other things she didn't even want to investigate just yet.

'The Neb's been shopping for you. That's a very bad thing,' Niffy informed her.

The Neb? Did Niffy Big Nose mean Mrs Knebworth?

'Because our housemistress is, let's be honest, the size of a beached whale, she thinks a fourteen is small. Your skirt will be massive,' said Amy, looking almost pleased at this.

'Just like mine.' Min held up a grey sack with box pleats which looked big enough to provide temporary shelter for a whole family. 'Don't worry, I've got safety pins.'

'OK, unpack, Gina, fair enough, but at least give us a clue as to why you're here,' Niffy urged. 'Then we'll show you round before supper.'

'Well . . .' Gina wondered what the shortest way out of this line of questioning would be. 'I guess . . . my mom was at this school and she wanted me to come here too, *for a little while*,' she added with emphasis.

Unfortunately this comment seemed to spark more interest than she'd expected.

'Your mum was here?' Niffy chipped in. 'Your mother is a St Jude's old girl?'

'Yeah.' Gina wasn't sure why this was quite so interesting.

'My mum was here too,' said Niffy. 'How old is

yours? Maybe they knew each other! That would be freaky.'

'Your mum came here all the way from California?' Amy sounded surprised.

'She's English,' Gina explained. 'Well . . . and half German.'

'She's German?' Amy asked in such a scornful way that it made Gina flush with annoyance.

'My mom's forty-four.' Gina looked at Niffy and pretended not to have heard Amy.

'Mine's forty-three. They must have known each other because the school was much smaller then. Was your mum a boarder?'

Gina nodded.

'What's her name?' Niffy asked

'Lorelei Winkelmann,' Gina said grudgingly, hating the idea that there might be some sort of connection between her and this weird girl.

'Lorelei Winkelmann! Yes, I've seen her!' Niffy exclaimed. 'Definitely! In one of Mum's old school photos. You don't forget a name like that. Plus she looked really out of place: crazy bleached blonde hair and masses of eyeliner. That's her, isn't it? Stuck out like a sore thumb and was obviously way too cool for school.'

Now Gina was relieved. Niffy didn't know anything about her or her mother. She was totally wrong, and Gina was going to enjoy telling her so. 'No way,' she said. 'Not my mom. No way.'

Gina thought of the school photos she'd seen of her mother, all mouse-brown hair and plaits. 'She was your regular straight-A student,' she added. 'She's real clever and I bet she was real boring at school.'

But Niffy looked back at her defiantly and asked, 'Are you sure?'

'Of course I'm sure! She's my mom, isn't she!'

'Well, there must be loads of things I don't know about my mother,' Niffy said. 'I think we'll have to do a search of the Banshee office archives one day – find out more about the intriguing Ms Winkelmann.'

'*The Banshee?*' Gina had to ask, although she felt slightly outraged that this girl could look up her mother.

'Banshee Bannerman, our headmistress. Banshee: a wailing Irish fairy, harbinger of doom. Don't worry – you'll catch up.' Niffy was unfolding her long legs, but her interest in Gina did not seem to be waning. 'So your mum now lives in California – doing . . . ?'

'Computer stuff,' Gina filled in.

'Cool. And she's decided to inflict St Jude's on you,

31

maybe so you can get some idea of what she went through.'

'Maybe.' Gina was not going to offer any further explanation about her home life to this irritating stranger. 'I'm only going to be here a term,' she reminded them all, certain in her mind that this was true. She'd do nothing but work and work. Get the grades and be out of here – maybe even by half term.

'So, to recap on the Daffodil dorm Easter holiday experience,' Niffy began, a grin spreading across her face, 'Min went home to Durban, wore her sari and her hair long . . .' This brought a laugh from Min, who was now in jeans and sweatshirt, plaiting her hair together.

'She ate fantastic curries twice a day,' Niffy continued, 'and listened to lectures from her doctor dad about how great it is to be a doctor and what a great doctor she'd make.'

'And doctor mum,' Min chipped in, rolling her eyes. 'Plus I babysat. I did a lot of babysitting. I have four little brothers and sisters,' she added for Gina's benefit, 'and we're all going to be doctors. That's the Singupta family plan.'

'I drank a lot of water too,' she went on, 'because home food is so hot after boarding-school food, and I listened to talk and more talk about promotions at the hospital and the latest weddings.'

'Instead of hanging out at the flash new riverside penthouse in Glasgow, Amy flew first class to Dubai,' Niffy continued, 'and turned mahogany by the five-star pool while her dad pursued a "great new business opportunity".'

'Yeah . . . a business opportunity dressed in head-to-toe Dolce,' came Amy's reply. The colour and glamour of her 'holiday' (tagging along while her dad considered buying a nightclub in Dubai City) was still so bright in her mind that the boarding house looked particularly dingy by comparison.

'And she dreamed of the gorgeous Jason Hernandez,' Niffy went on, 'and the day when he will finally sweep her into his arms and offer to be hers for ever.' There was no mistaking the tease in her voice.

'Oh, please, put a sock in it!' was Amy's response.

'And what about you?' Min asked. 'No, no, don't tell me: you spent three weeks at Blacklough Hall in the rain . . .'

Min thought with a slight shudder of the one and only visit she'd made with Amy to Niffy's 'ancestral' home. Blacklough had once been a splendid country mansion set in vast grounds, but now it was shabby and decaying; a place with terrifyingly big dogs, freezing bedrooms and threadbare carpets and curtains. Everyone had stayed huddled in the kitchen for the entire weekend, only venturing out once in a while to get soaking wet on a walk.

'You should come and stay with me in Durban – we'd have a great time,' Min had offered Niffy in sympathy as soon as the trip to Blacklough was over.

'Or me in Glasgow!' Amy had volunteered. 'You'd have your own bathroom – with underfloor heating and a Jacuzzi.'

'Were you riding Ginger?' Min asked now, 'or listening to your mum and dad's rows, or smoking behind the stables with your big brother?'

'All of the above,' Niffy admitted, thinking of the latest round of parental arguing. Glasses and vases had been thrown; furious threats of divorce had rung round the cold and crumbly corridors of the Hall.

'I'm so glad to be back at school. If only Ginger could be stabled nearby, then I could totally love it here,' Niffy admitted.

Amy's groan at this was interrupted by the loudest, most awful wailing alarm Gina had ever heard. Fire alarm? Air raid? She cowered with her fingers in her ears.

'Supper!' the other three girls explained.

'And I love school food,' Niffy added, springing up with enthusiasm.

Much later that night, Gina lay in her narrow bed, sleepless despite her jetlag, and listened to the breathing sounds of the other girls in the dorm. She had no recollection of ever having shared a room before – well, apart from sleepovers, when no one ever slept. Min gave a cough and turned over, causing her bed to creak.

'You asleep yet?' Niffy whispered. Gina didn't reply, sure that it wasn't aimed at her.

But then, still in a whisper, Niffy added, 'Gina?'

'Yeah?' Gina kept her voice low.

'Goodnight. Don't worry – it takes us a week or two to settle in again, and Amy and I have been here since we were ten. You'll take a while to get used to everything, but you'll get there.'

Ten?! Gina stared up at the shadowy, unfamiliar ceiling, wondering if she would ever get used to anything. There had been the supper, eaten at long tables in the dining room. Surrounded by the chatter of the ninety teenage girls who boarded at this school of 450 girls, Gina had picked at a plate of something she could only describe as glop.

'What is this?' she'd asked Min, mystified.

'Cheese-o-beano pie. Speciality of the house ... delicious!'

Gina had been able to identify orange beans and mashed potato, and she'd taken a nibble of the dark toast topping, only to choke on the weird salty taste.

'Grilled Marmite toast,' Min had explained, wolfing down another large mouthful. For such a dainty, petite little thing, she could really eat, Gina couldn't help noticing. Maybe she was bulimic . . . ?

Then there had been the Year Four sitting room – a beige and pink place with battered chairs and sofas, a TV no one switched on and a piano – where she'd met the other boarders in her year. A quick-fire of names and faces she hadn't a hope of remembering yet.

Strangest of all had been bedtime.

The wailing siren had warned them all that it was nine o'clock: 'Fourth Year's slot for the showers,' Amy had explained.

Gina had watched her roommates strip off, don dressing gowns and head for the bathroom. Once they'd gone, she'd undressed in privacy, put on her pyjamas and decided that, if there was a communal shower they all had to stand in together, she was calling her mom and flying home the next day.

Not that calling home was going to be easy. Cells weren't allowed (her lifeline home had been handed in!) and Niffy had told her about the elaborate queuing system for the boarding house's two pay-phones and three Internet computers.

'Basically, you're lucky if you get to make a call or pick up your email twice a week. That's why we have to resort to letters! Can you believe it! We're the last teenagers in the twenty-first century to still communicate by post!'

The showers turned out to have cubicles. There were also three private baths, but the rows and rows of sinks, towels and wash bags with name tapes in the bathroom had made Gina think of her personal pink bathing boudoir with utter longing. This was just so impersonal, so public. Where was she supposed to put on her make-up?

Close to 10 p.m., the loud screeching hinges of the fire door along the hallway had set Amy off on a countdown: 'Nineteen ... eighteen ... seventeen ...' And sure enough, as she reached one, the Daffodil dorm's door had opened and Mrs Knebworth, or the 'Neb', as everyone nicknamed her, had come in to wish them goodnight.

'Lights off in fifteen minutes and no later. We all

need our beauty sleep,' had been her parting shot.

'Some more than others,' Amy had muttered once the door was shut again.

'The Neb may seem friendly,' Niffy had whispered to Gina, 'but really she's the devil in disguise.'

Closing her eyes now and trying to summon up sleep, Gina felt a tear slide from the corner of her eye. Why had her mother sent her to jail?

Chapter Four

The wailing alarm had not just woken Gina but nearly sent her tumbling from her bed in panic at 7.30 the next morning. A frantic hour and a half followed: jostling for space in the bathroom, applying light make-up (on her bed with the aid of a compact mirror), dressing in the stiff new uniform and seeing immediately not just how horrible she looked, but how *wrong*.

Amy and Niffy's uniforms were well worn in and customized. Amy especially had found a way to make the individually hideous items at least slightly flattering. Her white shirt looked soft and comfortable and was unbuttoned low. Her sludgy cardigan was shrunken and bobbly, so it hugged her slim figure. Even better, her grey skirt was above the knee and worn with thigh-high socks and ballet pumps.

Gina suspected that just about every girl in Year

Four would be dressed like Amy, whereas Gina – in box-new, oversized clothes and woollen knee socks – would be labelled 'dork' before she even opened her mouth.

Once Gina had her entire enormous uniform on, complete with Min's safety pins to hold up the skirt, she angled the mirror on top of her chest of drawers to take a look at herself and was so horrified that, to her total embarrassment, she let out a muffled sob.

She looked much worse than any of them. Even Min, whose clothes were voluminous, at least still managed to look pretty.

'Erm . . . Are you OK?' It was Min who responded to the sobbing sound first.

'No!' Gina admitted. 'I am *not* OK. Look at this gross outfit!' She turned to them so they could take a better look at the full horror of it. 'I can't go out like this! People are going to laugh at me.'

And it was the thought of this – of a whole class full of strangers laughing and sniggering at her – that made Gina crumple down onto her bed, very close to a big, embarrassing, noisy crying outburst.

There was an awkward silence.

'Oh my Lord!' Niffy said finally. 'Well . . . there's no point in denying it. You look like a total twerp. Look at that skirt – it's nearly at your ankles! As for the cardie – you'd have to be built like Barbie to fill that one up.'

Although this wasn't exactly helpful, it did at least stop Gina's tears in their tracks. She wasn't ready to laugh with Niffy yet though.

Surprisingly, it was Amy who came to the rescue. Although yesterday she'd seemed pleased that Gina's uniform was too big, today she seemed to have had a change of heart. Maybe she understood an outfit crisis only too well.

'Just take everything off,' she instructed Gina briskly. 'You look about the same size as me, so you can borrow my spare things for the next few days, and at the weekend you can go to the uniform shop and change everything for smaller sizes. How about that?'

This was such a kindness, Gina's tears threatened to break out again, but fortunately they were nipped in the bud when Niffy added, 'You should be warned though, before you borrow her clothes, that Amy smells.'

'I do *not* smell!' Amy retorted angrily.

'You stink,' Niffy replied. 'You're always covered in melony, fruity, stinky stuff. Hair gel and body spray and all that kind of thing.'

Amy rolled her eyes and began pulling her spare school clothes out of a drawer for Gina. 'Funnily enough, not everyone wants to smell of horse and dog.'

As Gina gratefully took the much smaller clothes from Amy's arms, she clocked her totally bare face. Where yesterday there had been blusher, lipstick and eyeliner, today there was nothing but the gleam of moisturizer and lip salve.

'Is make-up banned?' she wondered out loud.

'Not exactly,' Amy told her. 'But no boys – so what's the point?'

Gina hadn't considered this. School with no boys. Not one. This was going to be a very new experience. School with no flirting, school with no crushes! But then again, school with no lame jokes, or fist-fights or truly terrible come-ons.

After they'd made their beds and breakfasted in the packed dining room, it was time to set off on the five-minute walk to the main school building.

'You are in 4C, aren't you?' Min checked. 'Same form as us?'

Gina nodded. They'd gone through the subjects they had in common last night. Everyone was doing English, maths, French, history and biology, but she and Min were taking chemistry and physics, while Niffy and Amy did art and Spanish.

'Shame,' had been Niffy's comment. 'Winding up Mrs Lexington-Harris, head of art, is one of the highlights of our week. But Min will look after you in physics – Mrs Wilson loves her. Min's her star pupil and Mrs Wilson already thinks she is' – her voice had dropped to a mock whisper – '*Oxbridge material.*'

'And what's that?' Gina had asked.

'Clever enough to get into Oxford or Cambridge University.'

'Oh yeah . . . right.' Gina *did* know what that was all about. Her own mother had already been bandying the words *Harvard* and *Yale* about, although Gina was quite obviously not even one of the cleverest girls in her class. Far from it. That was a big part of why she was at St Jude's, no doubt about it.

They crossed the boarding-house gardens and followed a path past several large playing fields to the main school. The great square stone building loomed up out of the grass. Four storeys high, with the top attic floors set into an immense slate roof, it was, Gina thought, much more imposing than it had looked in the handbook.

'How old is the school?' she asked Niffy, who was walking alongside her.

'Erm . . . early nineteen hundreds, I think. The first St J's girls wore hats, gloves, ankle-length pinafores and probably corsets. Can't have been much fun playing lacrosse in a corset.'

'I'm sure they didn't play lacrosse,' Min said. 'Far too unladylike.'

'Yeah,' Niffy agreed. 'They were too busy learning how to cook, sew and become perfect wives to Edinburgh doctors and lawyers.'

'Yeah, then at some point in the fifties,' Min went on, 'the school dropped the cooking and sewing classes and started teaching the girls how to become Edinburgh doctors and lawyers themselves.'

'My mum always said that one of the scientists who invented the Pill was from St J's,' Niffy added. 'But it's always been hushed up because it doesn't fit with the school's image. St J's is very, very proper.' She gave a roll of her eyes. 'They'd still make us wear hats, gloves, pinafores and corsets if they could.'

'What else should I know?' Gina asked.

But Min had a question: 'Should we be telling Gina to steer clear of Penny and her gang?'

'I'm sure she'll work it out quickly enough,' Amy

replied. 'Let's just put it this way. Every year has a set of poisonous bitches in it, and Penny, Piggy and Weasel are ours.'

'Piggy and Weasel?' Gina felt as if she needed some further clue to these girls than just the nicknames the dorm girls had given them.

'Tiggy and Louisa. Tiggy must be short for something, but no one ever calls her anything else, so who knows? I don't think you'll want to hang around long enough to find out. Unless you like the company of snobby Edinburgh bitches,' Amy added.

'Oh, they probably aren't that bad if you're a friend of theirs,' Niffy chipped in. 'It's just that Amy and Penny have never really got on. Penny once went out with someone Amy was considering chucking—'

'Yeah, but I hadn't!' Amy reminded her. 'He was still my boyfriend, that's the point.'

'And,' Niffy went on, ignoring the outburst, 'Penny has been at St J's since she was three and she'd got used to being the cleverest girl in the class and the best at everything. So when Amy arrived at the age of ten and started doing better than her at maths and art, not to mention Min turning up two years ago and being brilliant at physics and chemistry, Penny just went in a huff . . .'

'Yeah, and she's been in it ever since,' Amy added.

'Unfortunately 4C is quite small,' Min said, 'so it's a little hard to distance yourself from the three of them.'

Oh great, Gina was telling herself again. Didn't matter where in the world you went to school, there were always gangs. Another thought crossing her mind was that when she got back home, back to her real school, she was going to be so, so much kinder to new girls. It had never occurred to her before how terrifying it was to join a new class, make new friends, new enemies, find out where everything was and how everything worked all over again.

Because Min had been the first person to respond to her uniform crisis, because she seemed the nicest of the three and the geekiest and the one least likely to refuse, Gina – hating having to do this – turned to her and asked quietly, 'You will . . . um . . . be around today, won't you? Just to kind of show me where everything is? Won't you?'

Min smiled and nodded.

The words, 'I spy boarders,' greeted them as they walked into the classroom. They came from a tall girl with a pale, narrow face, a mane of long, curly brown hair and cruelly short fringe. She might have been pretty if she hadn't had the fringe and such a sneer across her face. 'Did you sleep well, girls, in your cosy little dorm? Ooh – and a new girl ... She's almost as tanned as you, Amy. Been to the Costas for a holiday, have you? Daddy got a little place in Benidorm?'

'Go away, Penny,' Amy growled.

But Penny held out her hand to Gina and said, 'Penelope Boswell-Hackett. How do you do?'

'Gina Peterson.' Gina shook the hand offered; she didn't feel as if she had much choice, although this was obviously the Penny she'd been warned about.

'So where are you from?' came the abrupt question.

'I'm just here for a term. I'm from the US ... California.'

'Oh dear,' replied Penny. 'Blonde *and* Californian ... good luck. Let's just hope you're not stupid as well. And you've had to borrow a uniform, you *poor* old thing.' And with that she turned on her heel and headed back to the far corner of the room, where a knot of girls giggled at her return.

Gina felt her face burning. 'Where do I sit?' she hissed at Niffy.

'Here, just take the desk beside mine.'

Gina sat down at the cramped, old-fashioned desk. She watched as Niffy lifted up the lid and began to unpack some belongings from her school bag into the belly of the wooden beast. This was like being at school in a different century. The room was pea-green with a scuffed wooden floor, a chipped iron monster of a radiator and two enormous windows, set high up in the wall. If a teacher in a long woollen dress carrying a cane had walked in, Gina would not have been surprised. She wondered if her mother had sat in this classroom once, and yet again she struggled to understand why her mother had wanted to send her to this place.

When the school bell rang at 8.50, an almost normal-looking woman came into the room and took the register. Gina tried to put names to faces, but gave up halfway through. It would take some time.

'Welcome back, girls . . . Welcome to our new girl, Gina Peterson . . . And off we trot to assembly,' the class teacher, Mrs Redpath, instructed.

Along with the rest of her class, Gina headed for the cavernous wood-panelled hall, already filling with hundreds of St Jude's girls. She followed Niffy and Min into a row of seats somewhere in the middle of the hall and picked up the small red hymn book on her chair before sitting down.

'You're about to see the Banshee in action,' Niffy

whispered. 'Pick a word, girls: *excellence, ambition, dedication* or *proud*. Person with the lowest score buys the treats on Friday.'

Gina had no idea what Niffy was talking about, but she heard Min choose *proud* and Amy *excellence*.

'Still chasing Jasey-Wasey, are we?' Penny, sitting in the row in front of them, turned round to direct this at Amy. 'Shame, because guess who I saw in the Harvey Nichols café stroking the beautiful hair of Camille from Year Five? Oh yes – one Jason Hernandez. And' – she paused for effect, arching one eyebrow – 'when I spoke to Camille afterwards, she said she wouldn't touch him with a barge pole because he's such a druggie.'

'Shh!' came the hiss from Mrs Redpath.

Niffy's hand went up to Amy's arm, as if to restrain her from making any reply, but it didn't help.

Amy spat out, 'And I suppose you think Llewellyn's such a saint, don't you? He's probably got his head in a bag of glue right now, along with all the other wasters from Burnside Academy. At least if Jason did drugs, he'd be able to afford the good stuff. But for your information, he doesn't.'

'I don't think you're quite in the same league as Camille though, are you? Little jumped-up

Glaswegian nouve,' came the vicious response.

Although Gina didn't know what this meant, she could tell from Amy's face that it was insulting.

'Penelope,' Mrs Redpath warned, 'turn round and be quiet!'

'See you later!' Penny muttered as she swivelled.

'Not if I see you first,' Amy hissed, adding for Gina's benefit, 'Like I'm supposed to be embarrassed that my dad comes from Glasgow and isn't a pompous lawyer. Cow!'

The piano struck up and the hall was filled with the sound of 450 chairs scraping wood as the girls got to their feet.

A loud burst of singing began. Gina looked at her neighbours, wondering which page to turn to, but found that no one was looking in the book. This was probably the school hymn and everyone knew it off by heart.

Niffy's version was clearly the unofficial one – something about lifting up your skirts on high so '*the king of glory enter may*'. She was shaking with suppressed giggles.

A severe-looking woman dressed in a dark suit and white shirt with wide lapels was striding in sensible court shoes towards the wooden lectern in the centre of the stage. Her short hair was swept back smartly and she had one of those complicated silver brooches pinned to her jacket that might as well have been a label reading: I'M OVER FIFTY AND TAKE MY POWER ACCESSORIES VERY SERIOUSLY.

'Banshee Bannerman,' Niffy announced. 'Count those buzzwords!'

'Girls,' the Banshee began. 'Welcome back for what I know will be a hard-working summer term. Our senior girls have their exams ahead of them. I know each and every one of you is going to make St Jude's proud.'

'Yess!' hissed Min. 'One–nil.'

'I know that your dedication to your studies will pay off . . .' the Banshee continued.

'Result!' Niffy hissed.

And on the Banshee went, racking up four points for Min, two for Niffy but still no score for Amy.

'Come on!' Amy was urging. '*Excellence* – we've got to have some *excellence* in here.'

'And now, girls,' the Banshee said, 'I'd like to introduce two new members of staff. First of all, one of our games teachers, Mrs Tweedie, has suffered an unfortunate car accident during the holidays. She'll be off for most of the term, but is expected to make a full recovery, so I'd like you to welcome

Miss Chrysler, who will take her place temporarily.'

As loud applause broke out for Miss Chrysler, Amy, Niffy and Min all turned to look at each other. 'Bum!' Niffy exclaimed. 'Here's hoping Miss Chrysler knows *something* about winning hockey and tennis matches.'

'Now the other news,' the Banshee continued once the clapping had died down, 'concerns our dedicated students of physics.'

Min leaned forward in her chair.

'I'm afraid Mrs Wilson has been called away from school for some time by an urgent family matter. However, we have organized a more than capable replacement who will continue to strive for excellence in this most important of departments.'

Just as Amy's face lit up – finally *excellence* had been uttered – Min's fell.

'Please welcome Mr Wilbur Perfect.'

'What!' Min gasped.

The loud clapping could not drown out the hilarity bubbling up from 450 girls who had just learned that their school staff now included a Mr Perfect.

'Mrs Wilson?' Min whispered. 'She's not going to be here? I can't believe it! Why didn't she tell me?'

Niffy whispered, 'Maybe she will, Min.'

'But,' Min began, 'I just can't get through everything without her!'

By the time the lunch bell sounded, Gina had lived through her first four classes at St Jude's. It had been tough going, especially the gruelling ninety minutes of 'double' French.

St Jude's seemed to specialize in teachers of the severe variety, who were determined to make learning as joyless as possible. And, boy, did they take class seriously here! There was no talking or time for anything fun, just heads down over the books and work, work, work. Gina didn't know if she was going to be able to stand it, let alone keep up. It wasn't like anything she'd experienced before. In her school back home, she was used to class discussions, group projects and a sense of 'let's find this out together'. Here it was just about listening to what the teacher told you: a boring information overload. And the girls all lapped it up without much complaint. She could understand now why everyone who came here did well.

The French teacher was actually French, which was kind of interesting. She wore a glamorous oyster Silk blouse a scarlet slash of lipstick and her hair up in a *chignon*.

As soon as Madame Bensimon spied new girl Gina, instead of doing something to make her feel welcome, she'd asked her to read a passage in French out loud – maybe so she could assess her. Gina had clearly heard the snorts and giggles coming from the other girls as she'd stumbled her way through the complicated text.

'*Hmmmm . . . très Americaine. Laid,*' had been Madame's verdict, '*Penelope, à vous.*'

That was the other thing: because Madame Bensimon spoke in high-speed French all the time, Gina struggled to make out any of her instructions.

But it became clear that she wanted Penny to read the passage again to show Gina how it was done. There was no mistaking Penny's smug and melodious French accent.

'*Bien fait,*' Madame had said at the end, gracing Penny with an indulgent smile. '*Merveilleux.*'

'She had a French au pair from the age of two and she holidays in France every year with her family,' Niffy had whispered to Gina. 'She's probably going to tell us that yet again.'

And sure enough, Penny had smiled back at Madame Bensimon and told her in fluent French that darling Paulette and summers in the Luberon meant she could now speak it almost like a native – although, *grace à* Madame Bensimon, her grammar was improving all the time.

At this, Amy had made vomiting actions.

Biology was hardly more fun. The girls had sat in long rows and copied furiously from the scrawled notes of a grumpy teacher, who seemed to have it in for Min.

'*Phylum*, Asimina – what do I mean by that word?' Mrs MacDuff had barked.

When Min had failed to come up with an answer, the teacher had snapped, 'Anyone intending medicine as a career will have to get a much firmer grip on the absolute basics, Asimina.'

'Yes, Mrs MacDuff,' Min had replied meekly.

After biology came physics, and as she approached the lab door, again Min had looked upset.

'I really liked to talk to her,' she said to her friends – Gina guessed she was speaking about Mrs Wilson, the absent physics teacher. 'She was like a mentor to me, not just a teacher. She really helped me. What can have happened in three weeks that's made her leave the school? She must have known before the holidays – I'm just so surprised she didn't tell me.'

Then the lab door had burst open and an extremely

tall man with jet-black hair and a bushy beard, wearing a white lab coat, had ushered them in with the words: 'Year Four, come in, welcome . . . I've heard so much about you all.'

Mr Perfect's Year Four class was small – only fifteen girls did physics – and in an unusual display of friendliness for a St Jude's teacher, he'd been determined to get to know everyone. He'd handed out blank paper badges, instructed everyone to add their names and pin the badges to their cardigans.

Spotting Min's name badge, he'd said, 'So you're Asimina . . . I have something for you.'

He'd gone to his desk, rummaged in the drawers and returned with a sealed cream envelope that had *Asimina Singupta* written across the front in loopy black letters.

Min had opened the envelope and taken out a two-page letter. She didn't reveal to Gina, Lucy or Suzie anything beyond: 'It's from Mrs Wilson,' but it seemed to have answered some of her questions about the teacher's departure.

During the lunch break, Gina sat uncomfortably with the boarders she knew and some of the day girls. Acutely aware that her presence was being tolerated rather than welcomed. But anything was better than sitting alone. Even answering excruciating questions like: 'Are you from Los Angeles?' 'Is your mum in the film business?' or 'Why are you here?'

Gina couldn't help noticing how much everyone ate. About five times more than Californian schoolgirls, even the ones without eating disorders.

Here, plates were piled high with baked potatoes, cheese, tuna and salad, and once the food had been demolished, almost everyone went up to get bowlfuls of sponge cake that came with a generous ladle of custard.

'Got to keep your strength up, newbie,' Niffy said, looking at the tiny helping of potato and salad Gina was still picking over.

Newbie?! What did that mean? Being new? Was that going to be her nickname?

'It's hockey after lunch. Our final lesson before the crucial last match of the season. And here's the goalie,' Niffy added when she spotted a muscular-looking girl with her blonde hair in a long ponytail striding towards their table. 'Hilary!'

It hadn't occurred to Gina that the girls would take hockey just as seriously as class here. All of them? Even Amy? These girls were all so hopelessly uncool. There was no way she was going to play hockey. Not today and not any day. She would ask to be excused because she knew nothing about the game.

Niffy and Hilary smacked their hands together in a high-five as Niffy asked, 'What's the plan? How do we demolish the opposition this afternoon?'

Chapter Five

Before leaving the boarding house that morning, Gina had stuffed her 'games' clothes into her brand-new gym bag without even looking at them, but now, in the chilly changing hut beside the playing field, she pulled out the items with something approaching horror. (It turned out hockey wasn't optional – she'd tried. Her request to Mrs Redpath had been met with the slightly withering: 'It's not as complicated as cricket, dear. Just join in and muddle along.')

There was a short-sleeved white shirt with tiny air-holes woven all the way through it; then came a pea-green sweatshirt with the school crest on the front, an enormous pair of navy-blue underpants, a boxy navy skirt and yet another pair of the evil woollen socks.

'Have you got boots?' asked Amy, already half undressed beside her.

'Boots?' Gina wondered. 'I put a pair of sneakers in here.'

'Well . . .' Amy looked doubtful. 'I suppose that will do for now. And a stick? There are a few spares over there behind the door.'

'A stick?' Gina felt anxious. She didn't want to be in charge of a stick.

'Don't you know *anything* about hockey?' Amy asked scornfully.

'No. Not a thing. Well . . . I've seen ice hockey on the TV.' Gina didn't want to add how terrifyingly vicious it had looked to her.

'Well . . . erm . . . maybe you should just try and stay out of the way for the first game or two, until you get the hang of things. That might be the safest thing to do. The sticks get swung hard and the ball is pretty solid. You don't want to get . . . clattered.' This came with a look which suggested that 'getting clattered' wasn't pretty.

Oh brother! Why hadn't her mom warned her about this? Maybe that had been the plan? To fly Gina halfway across the world and then have her killed by a hockey ball.

As she climbed into her stiff and voluminous new games clothes, Gina watched the other girls preparing for the match. Their short skirts were tucked into their blue pants, as if to get the material out of the way, their socks were pulled up to the knee, their battered boots laced on tight. Sweatshirts were tied on round their waists and hockey sticks were carefully scraped clean of old mud and polished up against their skirts. Were these just sticks? They were being treated like weapons. Hilary secured shin pads to her legs and rolled her socks on top of them, she pulled on a padded chest protector, tying it tightly, then buckled on a helmet and pulled the metal grille down over her face.

There was quiet in the room and serious intent in the air: the girls in here were evidently preparing for battle.

As they began to walk towards the hockey pitch, Niffy, clearly the captain, began to organize her team: 'OK, Hilary in goal, Min on the left wing, Suzie on the right. Amy and I will take the centre. Everyone else in the usual places . . . Gina?' Niffy seemed surprised to see her. 'Erm . . . we'll put you in defence – it should be quiet down there.' She couldn't resist a grin. 'The idea is to keep the ball away from our goal . . . Just try not to get in anyone's way, that's the main thing.'

Penny and her friends came out of another hut,

leading the other half of 4C onto the field. Gina began to feel slightly scared. This wasn't just about hockey, was it?

Miss Chrysler was already waiting on the pitch. As they got closer, Gina worried that she looked just a little too nice and too young and too fluffily blonde to really be in charge here.

'Hello, girls,' the teacher greeted them. 'Do you want me to put you into teams, or have you already picked?'

'We're sorted,' Penny replied.

'Well, why don't you play in the positions you want to first of all, and I can move you around, maybe make some changes as we go along?'

'Fine,' Niffy agreed. '*As if*,' she added under her breath. She started warming up her long limbs with squats and jumps.

It took a few moments for everyone to get into their positions, then Miss Chrysler blew her whistle and the game began. Gina, way down at the end of the field beside the goal, watched with wide eyes: she'd never seen girls do anything – apart from shopping in the sales – so vicious and ferocious before.

Sticks were smacking together, the ball whizzing across the field as the girls shouted at each other and thundered up and down, their studded boots sending clods of earth flying into the air. Every time the ball edged down towards her part of the field, Gina began to feel sick. She didn't even know which end to hold her stick by, but she didn't think any mistakes would be forgiven. If the ball came near her, she would at least have to try and do . . . something.

Amy and Niffy were charging up towards the far goal, walloping the ball to and fro between them.

'Come on!' Niffy was bellowing. 'I need some back-up!'

Weasel came running at Niffy with her stick down and there was a brief flurry before Niffy emerged with the ball.

Just as she blasted it over to Amy, who shot straight past the goalie's frantic block and into the corner of the goal, Weasel's arm went up and she shouted, 'Foul!'

Miss Chrysler's response was to confirm the goal and urge the girls to play on. 'Unless I see it and blow the whistle, don't stop,' she told them.

Penny and her team looked enraged, but play began again at a renewed level of fury.

Amy and Penny were wrestling with their sticks over the ball right in the middle of the field. They were wrestling over something else too.

'Aaaaaargh!' Amy was screaming in annoyance.

'Don't ever call my boyfriend a glue sniffer,' Penny shouted back, and raised her stick to take a swing that landed smack across Amy's shins.

'Owwww!' Amy shrieked, followed by, 'Leave Jason alone then!' as she got her stick behind the ball and made a run for it.

She passed straight to Min, who took off down the wing. Min could run, Gina thought. She could really run. Chunks of dirt and her long dark hair flew out behind her as she tore down towards the goal mouth.

As two players rushed out to tackle her, she shot the ball at Suzie on the opposite wing, who pinged it to Niffy.

Niffy cracked it hard, but this time the goal was saved.

'Bum!' she shouted.

'None of that please,' Miss Chrysler called out.

Now Weasel had the ball.

'On guard,' Hilary barked at Gina and Willow, the other girl in defence.

Penny was charging down the pitch towards the goal, ready for the ball, determined to score. Within seconds, the winger had passed to her and she was taking a mighty swing at goal.

Hilary ran out, kicked at the ball hard, but only managed to clear it by a couple of metres in – *no!!* – Gina's direction.

At the sight of the hard white object speeding towards her, Penny charging behind it, Hilary and Willow hot on her heels, Gina was tempted to turn and get out of there as fast as possible.

But very inconveniently, she remembered Penny's 'dumb blonde Californian' comment and knew that she had to try and stand up for herself. She closed her eyes, yelled and flailed wildly with her stick in the general direction of the ball. She heard a hard crack and then felt a second, softer kind of crunch.

When she opened her eyes, the ball was halfway down the field, which was a good thing, but Willow was standing in front of her with blood streaming from her forehead – which was not.

'Oh *no!*' Gina gasped. 'No, no! I am so, so sorry!'

Miss Chrysler blew the whistle long and loud and began to run towards them.

'Stick below the shoulder!' she was shouting. 'First rule of hockey! Stick below the shoulder!'

'I'm sorry – I'm so, so sorry,' Gina was repeating, both to Willow and to Miss Chrysler. 'I didn't know. I've never played this before.'

The blood was pouring freely down Willow's face; it was already at the collar of her white shirt.

When Miss Chrysler got her first full view of the injury, she was clearly panicked. 'Oh my goodness! Sit down, sit down,' she urged Willow. 'Oh my goodness,' she repeated, looking even paler than the injured girl. 'Are there any first aiders here? And can someone run for the nurse . . . *Run!*' she shouted.

One of Penny's wingers took off in the direction of the main school building.

'Min, you have to go over,' Niffy urged. 'New girl's decked Willow and you know the most about this stuff.'

Min began to trot towards Willow, but there was a reluctance in her sloping shoulders and bowed head.

Gina watched as Min came over and began to issue instructions without even looking directly at Willow. 'We need to lie her down, Miss Chrysler,' she said. 'Apply light pressure to the bleeding. Maybe we could use a sweatshirt, or paper towels.' At this request another winger shot off towards the changing huts.

Gina, who knew first-aid basics from camp, helped to ease Willow down onto her back. 'You're going to be OK . . .' she reassured her, but she felt as anxious as Miss Chrysler. This was all her fault.

'Where's the wound?' Min asked, kneeling close to Willow now, but with her head still held at a strange angle, as if she couldn't face looking at the injured girl directly.

'Her face – it's all over her face!' Miss Chrysler was close to tears and rapidly losing all credibility in front of the group of girls.

Min twisted her head and took a look, then jerked away again. 'Forehead, OK, that's fine. No soft tissue, loads of blood, but a surface wound.' She sounded impressively knowledgeable. 'Possibly concussion,' she added, 'but we've got to press on the wound lightly to slow the blood loss.'

The winger who'd gone to the huts was racing back with a great ball of paper towel in her hand. As Min stood up to take the paper from her hands, she seemed to buckle slightly and then just crumpled to the ground.

'Oh hell, there goes Min!' Niffy exclaimed.

'What on earth . . . ?!' Miss Chrysler shouted out.

By the time the school nurse had bustled out onto the playing field, she had two patients to care for. She briskly instructed several girls to support Willow as she walked to the first-aid room for treatment.

Min had to be cared for on the field. Gina worked

67

with the nurse as Min's legs were raised above the ground. Gradually she came round from her faint.

'What happened to you?' the nurse asked. 'Is it the sight of blood?'

Min nodded weakly.

'Dear, oh dear. Something to do with the vagus nerve, I believe.' She was patting Min's face with a wet paper towel. 'Often hereditary. Anyone else in your family keel over at the sight of blood?'

Min shook her head. 'Hardly!'

'OK, stay down here for at least five minutes, then your friends can help you back to the boarding house, where you're to take it very easy for the rest of the afternoon. Right, I need to go and see to the other casualty.'

The nurse treated the useless Miss Chrysler to something of a glare as she set off again.

Niffy and Gina linked their arms round Min's waist and shoulders to help her back to the boarding house; Amy accompanied them.

'Imagine being a games teacher and not knowing what to do with a bump on the head!' Niffy said indignantly. 'She was absolutely useless.'

'Totally,' Amy agreed. 'You were good though, Gina.'

'Oh no . . .' Gina shrugged off the praise. 'I feel so

bad. I had my eyes closed. I hit the ball without even looking!'

'You got her on the follow-through,' Niffy said, then added kindly, 'Don't worry about it. I'm sure she'll be fine. Cracking shot though!' She grinned at Gina.

'Yeah!' Amy agreed. 'I didn't think you'd be such a big hitter.'

'Oh . . . just luck, I guess,' Gina replied, but felt more than a little pleased at the compliments.

'We've only got one more house match, on Saturday, then the hockey season's over,' Niffy began. 'Willow's out, so I'm thinking, if we give newbie here a few tips, a little bit of practice, show her how to direct the swing . . . What do you think, Amy?'

Think about what? What were they talking about? Gina wondered.

'Absolutely,' Amy replied. 'Give it a go.'

'Gina,' Niffy began, grinning again. 'Welcome to the team!'

'*WHAT!*'

'And the gang,' Min said weakly from between them.

Chapter Six

'Mom . . . I'm not calling at a bad time, am I?' Gina knew that she probably was, but she'd had to take her chance on the pay phone when she'd been able to grab it.

'Oh . . . hi! Gina!' The voice on the other end of the line sounded surprised.

'Sorry . . . I just wanted to catch up with you all and it's hard to get to the phone here. Cells aren't allowed!' Gina still couldn't believe this.

'Oh . . . yes, I remember reading that now—'

'You knew that and you still let me come here?!' Gina was outraged.

'Well, anyway' – her mother didn't want to get into this – 'how was your first day at school, baby?'

'Just terrible,' Gina told her immediately. 'It's horrible. It's the worst place I've ever been to. When I say it's soooo last century, I really mean it. This place is frozen in time, Mom. I mean, there's a history teacher who is in her sixties! She's called Miss Ballantyne and I bet she was teaching when you were here. Wasn't she?'

'Miss Ballantyne?' Lorelei repeated. 'I don't remember . . . I don't think I remember the names of any of the teachers . . .'

'Really?' Gina pressed. 'Not one of them?'

'It was a long time ago,' Lorelei reminded her.

'So when is your idea of a joke going to be over, huh?' Gina went on. 'I'm really sorry I didn't study hard last semester, but I will make it up to you . . . Please, Mom, will you let me come home?'

When nothing but silence came back at her down the line, Gina wheedled, 'Pleeeeeease . . . Mommy?'

'It's too early to come home,' Lorelei told her firmly. 'You don't win your bet if you come home now, Gina. Just give it a chance,' she insisted. 'I think you're going to really love it.'

When Gina snorted at this, her mother added, 'Well, at least parts of it. Give it a chance.'

'I suppose you loved hockey, did you?' Gina demanded. 'You enjoyed running up and down wet grass with wooden sticks hitting a very hard ball around. It's deadly. I hit someone in the face in my first game and there was blood everywhere.'

'I'm sure you're exaggerating as usual.'

'I'm not!'

'How about class?' Lorelei was much more interested in this. 'How did you find that?'

'Boring,' Gina told her. 'But all the geeky girls here seem to love lessons – they can't stop studying all day long. They are weird – honestly, all of them. I don't think any of them has ever met a boy, ever.'

If Gina thought this was going to get her home early, she was so wrong. This was music to Lorelei's ears.

'Aha, Gina. Here's hoping some of that rubs off on you too,' she said.

'Huh!' It was all Gina could do not to slam down the handset there and then. Instead she managed to listen to her mother talk about Menzie and the fantastic weather and a few other things that made her feel sick to her stomach that she wasn't at home.

When the call was over, she stumbled out of the phone box and wondered where would be a private enough place to go and cry or at least shout and punch a pillow, but then Niffy ran down the corridor and tapped her on the shoulder.

'Got to come with us, newbie. Sideshow Mel's

first performance of the term. You can't miss it!'

'What?'

'C'mon, we'll get Amy out of the study room and go up.'

It wasn't difficult to tear Amy from her homework, then the three set off up the stairs past the warren of bedrooms, all different shapes and sizes.

'Mel's in Year Five and is the boarding house's resident sexpert,' Niffy explained. 'Well, she thinks she is. This is always good for a laugh, believe me.'

Gina followed them up the narrow staircase towards a door on the first landing, not knowing what to expect. Sexpert? No girl she'd met at St Jude's so far seemed likely to know the first thing about sex.

Niffy knocked on the door and announced, 'Hi, Mel, it's Niff and friends.'

'Come in!' called a voice from the other side.

Gina followed the girls into a tiny single room, where two other Year Four boarders were already sitting on the bed, while an older girl Gina guessed was Mel was perched on a chair in front of them.

'Come to find out what I've been up to on my holidays?' Mel asked. She was a strange-looking girl, thin but in a droopy way, not the lively, athletic thin of most of the other boarders. She had a large head with bushy dyed-blonde hair, and she'd painted thick circles of kohl around her protruding violet eyes.

'I have been such a naughty girl.' She grinned as Niffy, Amy and Gina scuffled round the room looking for somewhere to sit. 'I should charge for this information, I really should. You must be Gina?' she asked. 'The new girl?'

'Yeah,' Gina confirmed.

'Welcome to the boudoir. Now . . . I was just telling Flo and Minty about my new man – and I mean man, girls, *man*.' Mel held out her hands the required twenty centimetres or so apart, and both Flo and Minty began to giggle.

'Circumcised!' Mel whispered.

'No! And what did that look like?' Amy asked straight off.

Mel turned to her desk, rummaged for a sheet of paper and a pencil and obligingly drew two sketches on a sheet of paper. 'With and without,' she instructed, passing the paper around. 'It's useful to know these things.'

Gina studied the paper and wanted to laugh: both drawings looked ludicrously banana-shaped. If someone came at her with one of those, it would be impossible not to laugh hysterically.

But at least this was more like girl life as she knew it. Maybe St Jude's girls *did* know what boys were; maybe there would be a chance to meet some soon. Lovely though Aidan was, he was in California. Maybe there was someone over here who could take his place – in her daydreams at least.

'And what did you do with it?' Niffy asked with something of a disbelieving smirk.

'Well, since we were in the cinema, I told him to put it away till later,' Mel replied.

Amy gave a little snort of laughter at this, but Niffy persisted. 'And later?'

The violet eyes rolled slightly. 'Later, we had a little romp around on the sofa. He is such a good kisser. The best – absolutely no drooling at all. I feel a bit sorry for you, still having to go through the drooling and fumbling stage.'

At these words, 'Squid Boy' popped up in Gina's mind: she quickly nudged him out of the way with an image of Aidan, but then tried to block out Aidan too because any day now, she expected to get the news that he was Ria's new boyfriend. Well, she was in Scotland. Could she blame them?

'So, Brian—' Mel was saying.

But the name Brian brought peals of laughter from her audience.

'What's wrong with Brian?'

'Erm . . . everything?' Amy offered.

'Brian and I had a very nice little grope. He loves my breasts.' Mel looked down proudly at the two small bumps hidden under her school cardigan. 'More than a handful's a waste,' she added. 'Then my mum came in and said his taxi was at the door.'

'Did your mum see you?' Flo asked, slightly shocked.

'No, she knocked. I've trained her—'

Just then there was a sharp tap at Mel's door.

'Melanie Forsythe, what's going on in there?' said a voice on the other side.

'Just chatting – come in if you like,' Mel said loudly. In a whisper, she added, 'Lucinda alert.'

The door opened and two of the Year Sixes crammed into the tiny space: Lucinda and Maxine. Gina had already been warned about this pair of bossy rule-enforcers and saw that they didn't look too pleased at the sight before them.

'Not boasting to the little girls again?' Lucinda asked, managing to make both Mel and her audience feel insulted.

'No. We're having a cosy chat about our maths homework, aren't we?' Mel fired back.

'And so what would this be then? A visual aid?' Maxine bent down to the bed and picked up the sheet of paper with Mel's graphic graphics.

'Functions,' Niffy said breezily, as if it was the most obvious thing in the world. 'That's an upside-down bell curve' – she pointed at one of the drawings – 'and this' – her finger traced slowly over the second – 'is a steep parabola.'

She happened to know that neither Lucinda nor Maxine were studying further maths, so suspected she was on safe enough territory.

'Hmmm' – clearly Maxine wasn't convinced – 'your bed bell's about to go, so why don't you scarper off upstairs and leave us to Mel's romantic fiction.'

Gina followed the others out of the room. All the way up the stairs, they joked about Mel.

'A real *man*, girls,' Niffy mocked, holding out her hands half a metre apart. She burst out laughing. 'I don't know if I believe a single thing she says.'

'It's all true,' Amy assured her. 'She's a total slapper.'

'Five, four, three, two . . .' Amy counted under her

breath as Mrs Knebworth approached to bid Daffodil dorm goodnight.

The door swung open and the Neb stood before them, glowering at them in a way that was really quite worrying.

'Does anyone in here happen to know about the biscuit raid on the kitchen cupboards?' she boomed from the depths of her ample chest. Many a wasted handful was constrained with heavy-duty corsetry down there.

Four surprised and innocent faces turned to her at these words and hurried to say, 'No!'

'The main kitchen is out of bounds. Strictly and utterly out of bounds,' she told them sternly; then, in a different tone of voice, she asked, 'How was your first day, Gina?'

First of all Gina thought she should be honest and admit that this was all a terrible mistake and ask when the next flight for LAX was leaving. But there was something about the way Mrs Knebworth arched her eyebrows and focused her steely blue eyes, something about her rigid hair and sheer bulk, that made her terrifying. When she asked a question, there was no doubt that she was ordering you to give her the answer she expected.

'Erm . . . I'd say . . .' Gina began. 'I'd say it was all . . . pretty interesting.'

'Yes, I heard you laid someone out on the hockey field. Best to *swing low, sweet chariot*,' she added bafflingly. 'Good, good. Now, don't stay up too late, girls. Not healthy for the grey matter.' She tapped the side of her head.

As soon as she'd left the room, Niffy turned to Amy and asked, 'Did you?'

Amy smiled and nodded.

'Her special stash? Her personal supply?'

'Oh yeah.'

'When?'

'I always find the first five minutes of *Desperate Housewives* is the safest time.'

'You sneaky thief!' Min exclaimed.

If Gina had wondered what they were talking about, her answer came just as soon as Amy threw back her duvet to reveal four packets of biscuits in a variety of flavours: chocolate, chocolate orange, caramel crunch and jam-centred.

'Nice one!' Niffy told her.

In between mouthfuls of biscuit, Amy decided to get Gina up to speed with the entire sexual history of the dorm.

'I've snogged, obviously – that's kissing with tongues,' she added, not sure if 'snogged' translated into American, 'and had my boobs felt and just the tiniest bit of knicker-tweaking. Niffy's snogged and boobed, and Min, well . . . Min has her mind on higher things.'

Min snorted at this.

'What about you?' Amy asked, handing round the caramel crunches once again.

'Oh, snogging.' Gina said the unfamiliar word, then, because she was feeling just the tiniest bit more at home with these girls than she had the night before, she confided, 'I had this gross boyfriend – I only refer to him as Squid Boy because—'

But she didn't finish the sentence because her words were already drowned out by the groans and giggles of the others.

'Squid Boy!' Amy repeated. 'I don't think we need to know more! Soggy?'

Gina nodded.

'Slimy?' Amy asked.

Gina nodded again.

'Arms like tentacles?'

When Gina nodded to this too, Amy said, 'Don't worry. We've all been there. Plenty more fish in the sea—'

80

'Plenty more *squid* in the sea,' Niffy interrupted.

'And only four more days till the weekend,' Amy went on, ignoring Niffy. 'That's when we go fishing.'

'Watch out, Jason Hernandez!'

Chapter Seven

Amy and Niffy had spent an hour every evening out on the hockey pitch with Gina, practising before the match on Saturday morning. But now that the game was about to start and Gina was in her hideous games clothes, shifting her weight nervously from foot to foot as she stood close to the goal mouth, she didn't exactly feel confident.

Well, the practising had been fun . . . She had had a laugh with Amy and Niffy and had felt as if she was starting to get to know them better. But this was serious. Everyone here today wanted to win, that was obvious.

'Don't worry, you'll hardly have to do anything. We'll win,' Niffy had assured her before the start of the match. Their team was made up of some Year Fours and some Year Threes. Apparently it was something called a 'house' match: everyone in the school was in one of four different 'houses' which competed against each other.

'*Why?*' Gina had asked.

'I know,' Amy had agreed. 'Completely antiquated. It's not enough for us to have to compete against other schools, we have to compete against each other as well. But that's the St Jude's way: you're not doing anything useful unless you're winning.'

As this was the last match of the hockey season (postponed from last term because of flu, apparently), Niffy's team had to win it to secure the house junior hockey cup. 'But don't freak out,' Niffy had insisted to Gina. 'There's no pressure on you. We'll win.'

But Gina had found out that Penny's team had beaten Niffy's 3–1 in the house match last term, so she had continued to ask slightly desperately, 'Isn't there someone else who could do this?'

Niffy had just rolled her eyes. 'Year Three is full of weak-armed weeds,' she'd insisted. 'I need someone who can belt the ball up the field, if required. You're good, honestly.'

Before Gina could worry further about whether or not she should be there, the referee blew the whistle and, with a hearty thwack, the rock-hard ball was on the loose, with girls brandishing wooden sticks thundering after it.

Within moments, Penny had the ball and was moving at a terrifying rate towards Gina's end of the pitch. She crossed the ball deftly to Louisa and, with a lurch, Gina saw Louisa move skilfully towards goal.

Gina fumbled her stick and saw Penny charging towards her, shouting out, 'I'll get it! She's the new girl and she's useless!'

As the ball sped towards her, Gina realized it was a now-or-never moment. She had just a second or two to stop the ball and hit it away with all her strength or else Penny was going to take it from under her nose and score.

Gina's first thought was to throw down her stick and run as fast as her legs could carry her. She hadn't wanted to be in the stupid team anyway. She couldn't play this dumb game! If she was totally honest, she was only here because she thought it might help her make friends with Amy and Niffy, but now she saw that it was much more likely that they would never speak to her again. Because she was going to mess up!

Then Penny, still running, began to laugh. Feeling a rush of anger, Gina made her decision. She wasn't going to run; she was at least going to try.

She swung her stick as hard as she could. There was a crack as she made contact with the ball. But the rebound, which shot up into her hands, made her drop the stick in pain.

'Ow!' she couldn't help wailing as she tucked her smarting fingers under her arms.

'Dangerous play!' Penny was shouting, and Miss Chrysler was blowing her whistle. All Gina could see was Niffy's thunderous face. Although the ball was right up at the other end of the field, clearly Gina had not done a Good Thing. She suspected her stick had gone above her shoulder again. And hadn't Niffy warned her about this? 'It's not frigging golf!' she'd told her.

In the blurry moments that followed, Gina was sent off; Penny was awarded a free shot and scored, making it a terrible 1–0.

It was nearly an hour later when Amy and Niffy returned to the dorm to find Gina sulking angrily.

Before they could even get out a word about how the rest of the match had gone, Gina let rip. 'Don't blame me! I never want to be in your team again! I didn't want to be in it in the first place! It was a really bad idea. I just felt guilty about Willow.'

Both girls just smiled at her.

'Don't worry,' said Amy. 'You're right.'

'We were desperate, newbie,' Niffy agreed. 'But it's OK,' she added, her smile spreading further.

'Oh!' Gina got it. 'You totally won, didn't you?'

'Yes!' they both replied together, and Niffy gave some sort of bizarre little victory jig.

'You total daftie.' Amy laughed at Niffy.

'It was a good shot,' Niffy assured Gina. 'You've got very strong arms. Do you do weights?'

'No. It's probably from tennis,' Gina told them, 'and swimming. We have a pool – and a court – at home.' For once she didn't say this boastfully: she didn't want to put these girls off. She was beginning to realize they were the only chance of friends she had in this dump.

'A tennis court?' Niffy asked, looking excited.

'Yeah . . . but it's not such a big deal over—'

'You play tennis?'

'Yeah?'

'Do you play well?'

'I'm OK . . . but just a minute . . .' Gina was suspicious. 'Don't tell me – there's a junior house tennis cup as well, isn't there?'

Niffy just nodded and said, as if to herself, 'We need

six: three pairs and two people good enough to play singles as well—'

'Don't even think about it!' Gina told her.

'Oh yes! The hockey season is now officially over and it's tennis from now on,' Niffy explained, stripping off her muddy and sweat-soaked games clothes and bundling them into her laundry bag.

'OK,' Amy began, 'the plan is we get showered and changed, then we take you out to see the many sights of Edinburgh.'

'We're allowed to go out?' Gina asked; she'd somehow thought they'd have to stay in the boarding house all weekend.

'Of course!' Amy laughed. 'We're allowed out at the weekend, by day and by night,' she added.

'Under carefully controlled conditions,' Niffy reminded her.

'Which we bend a little.'

'What about Min?' Gina wondered. 'Where is she?'

'In training,' said Amy. 'Look out of the window.'

The dorm's high third-floor window gave an eagle's-eye view of the school playing fields. The pitches were empty now, but on the athletics track there was a lone figure still in sports kit.

Min was pacing out distances and marking them with what looked like two water bottles.

'She's hoping to win the under-sixteens eight hundred metres on Sports Day,' Amy explained. 'She came third last year, so there's a good chance. But anyway, c'mon, scrub up, we're going shopping!'

'I can come with you?' Gina wanted to check, because going shopping with someone . . . it was kind of personal. Did Amy really want to invite her?

'Yeah. We'll show you round, newbie,' Amy replied. 'It'll be fun.'

'OK, here's the deal.' Gina turned to them with a determined look on her face. 'You have got to stop calling me that!'

'Six hundred and fifty quid for a handbag!' There was no mistaking the outrage in Niffy voice. 'A *handbag*!' She put the offending item back on the shelf. 'I'm sorry, Amy, but even you can't afford that.'

'Well' – Amy tossed her blonde hair, knowing perfectly well they were within earshot of the sniffy sales assistant – 'if I wanted to use up my entire term's allowance on one fabulous investment piece, I could.'

'Get lost,' Niffy told her. 'Six hundred quid? You could buy a horse for that.'

'Yes, I'm sorry, but we're in Harvey Nichols,' Amy snapped, 'not Pony World.'

Niffy snorted in a very horse-like fashion.

'Come on,' Amy instructed. 'Let's go and buy some make-up.'

Ever since they had got off the bus . . . OK, *that* had taken Gina by surprise.

'We're going by bus?!' she'd asked the others. 'Is that OK? I mean . . . will we be safe?'

Back home, when Gina went anywhere, she was taken by car, which usually meant there was a parent on hand wherever she went. Buses were for crack addicts, muggers and beggars, or so she'd been given to understand.

The idea of three girls just jumping onto a bus and travelling into town was . . . terrifying.

But Niffy and Amy looked at her in astonishment.

'Safe?' Niffy laughed. 'Unless you think toddlers or little old ladies in hats are dangerous, then yes, it is safe!'

But as soon as she'd stepped off the bus and in through the shiny revolving glass doors of Edinburgh's chicest department store, Gina had felt just ever so slightly at home.

Unlike the boarding house, with its screaming

alarm and weird food and communal bathrooms, unlike school, with the bitching and the hockey and the uptight teachers, Harvey Nichols was a place Gina immediately understood.

This glossy consumer paradise was all about clothes and shoes and shopping. Here, just like at home, she could linger over the expensive shampoos and luxury lipsticks, and then treat herself to an overpriced latte. Here, she got it. For the first time since she'd arrived in this strange Scottish city, she felt herself relax.

Considering they came from opposite sides of the globe, Amy and Gina were dressed in remarkably similar fashion. They were wearing their latest shopping outfits: tight jeans, flat pumps, complicated jackets and bags (Diesel and Mulberry for Amy, Nordstrom and Coach for Gina). Amy had wound a thick pink and silver scarf around her neck and applied too much blue eye shadow. Gina had overdone the bronzing powder and had picked a buttercup-yellow top, which would have worked in sunny California but was too strident for the cool grey of Edinburgh.

Niffy was the one who looked out of place in this shopping Mecca. She was wearing scuffed riding boots, oversized jeans and a big beige mac. Although it was Saturday and there was every chance of bumping into the male of the species round every corner, Niffy's only concession to make-up had been the application of Vaseline to several nasty lip cracks.

While Amy and Gina bonded over Aveda blushers ('This one's nice – not too pink, not too red'; 'Mmm . . . yummy'), Niffy continued with her diatribe: 'This bottle of shampoo costs twenty-eight pounds – they're having a laugh!'

'Could you just shut up?' Amy hissed, her patience finally snapping. 'You're a flaming bumpkin! You sound like my gran. And you know what? You could probably do with some of that! Look at your rat's nest!'

Amy took Niffy by the shoulders and turned her to face one of the store's mirrors, so she could examine her curly mop, bundled up into a scrunchie.

'Jason could be here – he could be in this shop, we could bump right into him and I'll be with you, mop-head! Flapping about in your mac, looking like a scarecrow!'

'Oh, this is all about Jason, is it?' Niffy replied, but her eyes hadn't left her reflection and it was hard to miss the hurt expression on her face.

'Don't, Amy,' Gina broke in. 'Niffy looks fine.'

'What about the trial size?' Amy's voice sounded a little less angry. 'Why don't you get the trial-size shampoo and conditioner for curly hair? Honestly, it's really good. No! You know what?' As Amy took Niffy by the arm and led her round the corner, Gina recognized the zeal of a true fellow shopper.

'Ta-da! This is the shampoo for you,' Amy announced in front of the display. 'Barielle shampoos, conditioners and nail care made from' – she flourished a bottle under Niffy's nose – 'hoof oil.'

'Really?' Niffy exclaimed with enthusiasm. 'Does it smell the same?' She began unscrewing the lid of the bottle.

'Oh, no doubt!' Amy rolled her eyes.

When Gina handed her credit card over to the woman behind the till, she hoped her mother wouldn't mind too much.

'You'll have to get some warmer things,' Lorelei had warned her, after all. 'Even though it's summer, summer in Scotland isn't like anything you're used to. Let's put it this way – you won't be needing your bikini, or the factor forty.'

Gina's purchase of two pairs of very expensive

jeans, two DKNY tops and a cute red jacket from Whistles had impressed Amy.

'I'm going to get one of those tops too,' she decided. 'You don't mind, do you? We'll just wear them on different days.'

'Sure, no problem.' Gina had smiled at her, and suddenly Amy was her new best friend because this was just like going to Nordstrom's with Ria and arguing about who was going to buy the pink one and who'd have to get the blue because they both adored it so much.

When the shopping was over, it was time to ride the escalators up to the café on the top floor.

'We'll go to the toilets first,' Amy instructed. 'Check ourselves over. This café is really popular – everybody comes here . . . anybody could be here,' and they knew exactly who she was thinking of.

In Amy's mind, the scene was playing. She would emerge from the Harvey Nichols toilets, hair freshly brushed, lip gloss applied, looking as gorgeous as possible. She would round the corner into the café and there, bathed in the late afternoon sun streaming in through the huge windows, would be Jason, alone, sipping moodily at a cappuccino (or did he drink espresso?). Well . . . no matter. He would look over, see her, smile and say, 'Amy' – yes, he'd remember her name – 'hello there! You're looking great. Come over and join me.'

Instead, as Amy emerged from the toilet, all fragrant and fluffy, rounded the corner into the café and scanned the sunny room in hope, she heard a nasty mocking voice call out, 'Oh look! Someone's let the boarders out! Are you sure you've got time for a coffee, girls? You don't want to miss the bus and be late back.'

Penny revolting-Boswell-totally-revolting-Hackett. Complete with Piggy and Weasel and two boys, one of which had to be Penny's *state school* boyfriend, Llewellyn.

Amy had a split second to decide which would be worse: turning and leaving, so allowing Penny to laugh and feel she had the upper hand; or staying here and having to endure the snide glances and even snider remarks from the other side of the room.

'Table for three,' Amy told the waitress defiantly. 'As far away from the window as you can, please.'

'He's not here, you know,' Penny sang out as they walked past her table.

Amy turned her head and glared.

'Been spending some of Daddy's cash?' came the

sneer. 'Dressing up later, are you? Or won't you be allowed out again?'

'Come on, Amy.' Niffy ushered her along, giving Penny just the merest snooty nod of acknowledgement.

'A little overdressed for the cinema, aren't we?' the Neb commented as Amy, Niffy, Min and Gina came into her sitting room to sign out for the evening, wearing a colourful mix of denims, bright skirts and tops, strappy shoes, make-up, latest hairstyles and room-filling perfumes. Gina was in her new jeans, Amy her new top, and both of them had worked hard to dress up, make up and generally style the more fashion-challenged Niffy and Min.

'It's a natural reaction to wearing sludge-green all week,' was Amy's defence.

'So what are you going to see? And where? And will you be back by ten thirty and not one moment later? In a taxi?' the Neb wanted to know.

Mrs Knebworth was in her armchair, still neatly clad in a tweed skirt and satin blouse. She made no dressing-down concessions to the weekend. Some of the boarders staying in tonight were nestled on sofas and floor cushions all around her because they were actually going to watch a film with *her*. Just the thought made Amy and Niffy's toes curl.

Min was primed to answer. She'd done the Internet research: she knew the times, the cinema, the in-depth on-line reviews of the film they *weren't* going to see tonight. They had something much more interesting planned instead, but going out on café crawls was banned, as the Neb suspected, quite rightly, that this might lead to the two evils it was her job to guard the girls against: *boys* and *drinking*.

'*The Girlfriend Project*, up at Tollcross,' Min informed her. 'And yes, we'll get a taxi there and a taxi back.'

When their cab pulled up at the boarding house, the girls climbed in, then passed the fifteen-minute journey twitching and twittering.

'Is my hair OK?' Amy wanted to know, running her hands over it for the hundredth time.

'Fine,' Niffy told her, but although Niffy had been her best friend since their first day at St Jude's, Amy looked to Gina for expert reassurance.

Gina fished a wide-toothed comb out of her bag and smoothed over the back of Amy's long locks.

Min held her feet up to examine the red mid-heels

she'd borrowed from Amy for the night. 'They're lovely but we can't walk too far, OK?'

Niffy, who'd finished her outfit off with long, flat brown boots, just snorted at this.

The excitement in the air was infectious. Gina could feel a little tingle of nerves starting up in the pit of her stomach. She wondered how different Edinburgh boys would be from the ones she hung out with back home. She was bursting with curiosity. Where were they going to find them? What would the cool places be like here? Gina had faith in Amy.

Amy had showed her a picture of Jason. It was kind of blurry, downloaded from the St Lennox website, but he was undoubtedly good-looking, and so were lots of the other boys in the team photo. They looked clean-cut and preppy-ish.

The black cab dropped them not outside the cinema in Tollcross but in George Street, right in the centre of town, where the bars, cafés and restaurants were gearing up for the busy night ahead. Ideal territory to start hunting for the gangs of boys the girls knew would be out and about tonight.

As Gina was beginning to understand, far from having no boys in their lives at all, the St Jude's girls knew boys from every other single-sex private school in town. Inter-school dances, dancing lessons, theatrical performances and debating competitions were ways in which the schools socialized formally; hanging out at weekends was how the girls met the boys informally.

'OK.' Amy took charge of the group. 'I have a list of places to try, but some of them are over-eighteen only.'

Something, she had to acknowledge, that was going to be a problem. She and Gina might just about get away with it, but Min and Niffy, with their girlish faces – not a hope.

'Oh, I'm not doing that!' Min insisted, crossing her arms. 'We could get expelled!'

'Rubbish!' Amy exclaimed. 'Who's going to tell? Well, you'll have to wait outside then . . . Maybe Nif can keep you company,' she added hopefully.

'Me?' Niffy sounded hurt.

'So you've not actually arranged to meet anyone?' Min asked in surprise.

'Well, not exactly, but I sort of know where some people might be,' Amy replied defensively.

'I hope this isn't going to be a total waste of time . . .' Min huffed. 'I wish we were just going to the cinema.'

'It's a hunt, Min – thrill of the chase. Where's your sense of adventure?' Niffy asked. 'Anyway, that film's supposed to be terrible.'

'Everyfilm dot co dot uk gave it three stars.'

First on Amy's hit list were two cafés, one in a late-night bookshop. 'We'll just go in and look around. If there's no sign of anyone interesting, we'll head off,' she told the others. 'No point buying a coffee in every place. We'll be wired.'

'And skint,' Niffy pointed out.

At the first café there was no one they knew and nothing happening, so they left just as quickly as they'd gone in. At the second, they were greeted enthusiastically by four boys crowded onto a small table close to the door.

'Amy, Niffy and Min!' one of them called out. 'You've been sent by our fairy godmother to make the evening more interesting! Come over here and talk to us. It's been ages! How were the holidays?'

'These are guys from Jason's year!' Amy whispered to Gina as they went over. 'They might have info! Might know where he is.'

Gina studied the group of boys. With their sleek hair, good teeth and big smiles, they looked just like the guys in the team photo. A very handsome gang.

'Hello, you must be new. I'm Angus.' The boy who'd called them over held out his hand to Gina, who took

99

a moment or two to work out that he wanted her to shake it.

'Hi there, Angus,' Gina said, taking his hand with a smile. 'This is very formal. We don't really do this where I come from.'

'You're a Yank!' Angus responded and stuck his hand in the air. 'C'mon then, we'll do a high-five. This is Pete, Milo and Jenks, by the way.' He gestured to his friends. 'They'll probably want to slap your hand too.'

'I like it!' Niffy grinned and pulled up a sleeve. 'Much better than kissing on the cheeks.'

'Hey,' Milo intervened. 'Don't knock kissing on the cheeks – it's as close to snogging as Pete is ever going to get.'

'Hey!' Pete couldn't stop himself from blushing.

'Why is the scary girl rolling up her sleeve?' Milo asked, pretending to sound frightened.

'I think she's going to go round the table and punch everyone hello,' Min told him.

More chairs were brought over, until the eight of them encircled the tiny table.

'We'd offer to buy you coffees, but we've all had grande lattes and paninis, so now we're broke.' Angus gave an apologetic smile.

'Mortgaged!' Pete added.

'Oh, we weren't going to stay long,' Amy replied. When Angus pulled a long face at this, she added quickly to spare his feelings, 'We've got a film to go to.'

'We could come!' he suggested brightly.

'Rom com,' Amy said quickly, to put him off.

'And you're supposed to be broke,' Niffy reminded him.

'Oh yeah – that's a point,' he said.

After some more chat, Amy, trying to sound as casual as possible, asked them, 'So . . . who else is about tonight?'

'Aha . . . And I suppose that means: where is the gorgeous Jason Hernandez?' Angus understood straight away.

'No!' Amy insisted, but all four boys and Niffy began to laugh.

'What you need to know,' Milo chipped in helpfully, 'is that Jason said he might go and catch something at the Filmhouse or he might just hang out at the Arts Café.'

'Tricky.' Jenks leaned forward to join in the discussion. 'Those places are at opposite ends of town . . . so which one are you going to pick? Or would you like me to get out my mobile' – he removed the phone from his pocket with a flourish – 'and ask Jason directly?'

'No, no,' Amy insisted, imagining Jenks dialling Jason, then saying something as gruesomely embarrassing as: *I've got Amy here – she wants to know where you are tonight . . . Why? Because she's in love with you. Everyone knows that.*

'Well . . . we should be going,' Amy said, taking a deliberate look at her wristwatch. 'Our film starts at eight fifteen.'

'Aha, and that'll be at the Filmhouse, I suppose,' Jenks teased.

'No,' Amy fired back.

'You can't go just yet,' Angus pleaded. 'I've not said one word to Nif.' He turned towards her and said jokingly, 'Hello, old girl. How's your brother? And the dogs? And the horse? Tell me everything.'

Then, when Amy repeated that they really should be going, Angus turned to Gina. 'And what about your new American girl?' he complained. 'I've not even had a chance to meet her. Where in the US are you from?'

'California,' Gina replied, leaning forward in her chair to get a little closer to him: he was definitely cute-ish.

'Nice . . .' Angus replied, then struggled for what to say next. 'The Beach Boys!' he blurted out.

'The Beach Boys! Well . . . yeah . . . that was a while ago, I guess.'

'We really should go.' Amy stood up and gave Gina a nudge.

As the four girls started towards the café door, after high-fiving everyone goodbye, Angus couldn't resist singing, unbelievably tunelessly: '*I wish they all could be California girls.*'

Once they were out on the pavement again, the girls set off along George Street in the direction of the Filmhouse, giving Gina a detailed commentary on the boys they'd just met.

According to Amy, Angus was 'very sweet. He used to go out with some girl in Year Five'. Pete was 'a little bit of an airhead, into playing the guitar'.

'Milo's nice,' Min offered, and earned herself a round of laughter and whistles. 'I didn't mean it like that!' she insisted, totally flustered.

'Jenks is pug-ugly and more annoying than a rash,' Amy stated.

'That's not very nice!' Niffy argued, and started the laughs and whistles up again.

Gina decided to offer an opinion of her own. 'I thought they were all kinda cute and kinda fun. Isn't it just such a shame that they're not at school with us? Don't you think class would be so cool with them in it?'

But this was so way beyond the imagination of the three other girls that they couldn't even reply.

At the end of George Street they walked through the kind of quaint black-stoned, brass-lamped Georgian square that Gina had only previously seen in costume dramas screened on the Public Broadcasting Service.

'Wow!' she kept saying, to everyone's complete indifference. 'Look at the lamps! And the railings! Wow! It is so beautiful here. So historical.'

Niffy began to giggle, then Gina made everyone laugh by declaring, 'Wow!' another three times and then finishing off with an enthusiastic 'I'm all out of wows!'

They turned into noisy, lively Lothian Road, where groups of teenagers were shouting at each other, bars over-spilling onto the pavements and queues forming at the pizza takeaways and chip shops.

The Filmhouse bar was packed, every seat taken, the serving area two-deep with students in macs or leather jackets, glammed up schoolgirls and the grown-up culture-vulture types the place attracted.

'I think we should have a drink here and just hang out a bit,' Amy told them as she sidled through the crowd, scanning the room as carefully and yet as subtly as she could.

'There on the left! Down near the bar! Look, Amy!' Niffy hissed at her.

The girls all turned their heads and Gina saw, not the tall, handsome, raven-haired sixteen-year-old boy she'd been told to look out for, but instead the bossy sixth formers, Lucinda and Maxine, laughing over a joke with friends.

'Duck,' came the instruction from Min.

Although they were still in a crowd and probably wouldn't have been spotted by the Year Sixes, all four dropped to their haunches and began to back slowly out of the bar and towards the double doors.

They should have made a swift getaway, except the double doors flew open and Niffy, still hunched down, still moving rapidly backwards, crunched straight into someone coming in.

'I'm so sorry,' she apologized, turning round but not yet daring to stand up straight.

The sound of the voice that replied made Amy blush right from the balls of her feet up to the roots of her lavishly highlighted hair.

'No problem – but what are you all doing down there? Oh hi, I know you, don't I? Amy, isn't it? From St Jude's?'

'Yes, hi . . . Hi, Jason.' Amy swept her hair from her face, set her smile on full beam and stood up to greet him, wondering why she had to be doing something as stupid as crawling backwards out of a room just as she almost literally bumped into him. 'Down here?' she repeated, wondering what on earth to say. 'We're just, erm . . .'

'Min's dropped a contact lens,' Niffy said as she began to pat gently at the carpet. At these words, Amy made a promise to herself that she would never say an unkind thing about Niffy's hair ever again in gratitude for this sensational explanation.

'Oh dear.' Jason dropped to his knees and began to pat at the carpet as well.

All five of them were circling the space, as the girls sneaked little peeks at this current legend of the dorm. He was so good-looking – no doubt about it. Liquorice-black hair, the longish side of short, olive skin, thick eyebrows and full straight lips that led with a curve to a straight, slightly flared nose. He wasn't just handsome though, he was also kind of fabulous. His scuffed leather jacket was cool, his shirt collars flopped just so and his caramel suede boots looked exactly right.

Amy wasn't the only one whose heart was beating too fast. But they were all wondering who was going to call a halt to the contact lens charade.

'You know, it's not really a big deal – they're weekly ones. I would have thrown it away in a few days anyway,' Min said, finally releasing them from the pretence.

'Oh, right . . . That's probably a good thing then, because I think my film's about to start.' Jason turned his wrist to glance at an expensive-looking steel diver's watch.

'Oh!' Amy gasped, and there was no mistaking the disappointment in that single syllable. 'What are you going to see?' She straightened up, no longer caring if Lucinda and Maxine could spot her.

'*Le Terminal* – it's a horror film set in an Algerian airport.'

A quick glance at her friends' faces told Amy that no matter how deeply in love she was, they were not going to sit through a slasher flick in Algerian just so she could take furtive glances at Jason's perfect profile.

'Where are you headed?' Jason asked. 'Somewhere fun?'

'Oh . . . erm . . . the Arts Café, you know . . . at the Institute?' Amy said, making use of her inside information that this was one of his hangouts.

'Yeah . . . well, never know, I might come along later. Right, well . . . see you.' And with a turn of his handsome head, he was gone.

'The Arts Café is miles away!' Min hissed at her. 'The other end of Princes Street! There's no way I can make it there in your shoes. My heels are already bleeding!'

'We'll get a taxi and I'll pay,' was Amy's solution. 'We've got to get out of here asap,' she added. 'Year Six is on the move.'

'So what can I get you girls?' The Arts Café waiter was at their table with a notebook and pencil, smiling in a very friendly way.

'Niffy, we're having wine, aren't we? Red?' Amy asked with confidence. She might be a full three years below the legal age to buy drink, but this was a culture café – you could usually get away with ordering wine without an age check. That's why so many of their friends came here.

'Min? What would you like?' she asked. 'Gina?'

Both girls, much less willing to break the law

as well as the school rules, plumped for cappuccinos.

'Erm . . .' The waiter paused. He didn't look much older than sixteen himself: skinny, tall, with sandy hair and a white shirt so flimsy they could see clean through to his nipples. With his black trousers, he looked as if he was in school uniform, minus the tie.

'I don't know if I can do wine for you . . . erm . . . because' – he leaned over the table towards them conspiratorially – 'well . . . *if* you're under twenty-one, and I'm not saying you are, I'd need to see some ID. And not everyone carries their passport around with them all the time these days.'

'Fine, fine.' Amy knew she was being offered the chance to back down gracefully. 'Shall we have coffees too, Niffy?'

'Irish coffees?' Niffy dared him with a smile.

'Two Irish coffees? Well . . .' The waiter shot her a cheeky little grin back. 'I don't see the harm in that,' he told them. 'Medicinal purposes.'

'Exactly,' Niffy agreed.

When he'd hurried back to the bar with their orders, Amy told the group, 'Ooh, I like him. I was just about to ask him his name, but—'

'Let me guess,' Niffy interrupted: 'he's wearing the wrong kind of aftershave? No, his shirt – it's his shirt. You don't go out with people in white shirts.'

Amy shook her head. 'Nothing wrong with a nice white shirt, *which isn't see-through*. No, it's the trainers. They're white. Completely white.' She turned to Gina to explain while Min and Niffy just rolled their eyes. 'White trainers are a no-no. I just don't go there. It always turns out badly. But you know, if Jason doesn't show,' she added, applying lip gloss carefully with a little brush, 'it's good to have a back-up.'

'If Jason turns up here when his film finishes, I'll do all your dishwashing duty for the rest of the term,' Min promised. 'That's how likely it is.'

Amy just sighed in reply, but cheered up a little as the waiter returned with a tray of coffees.

'What's your name?' Amy asked him with her glossy pink smile in place.

'Dermot O'Hagan, at your service. And ladies, what may I call you?'

'Miss,' Amy joked.

'Oh, I see. It's like that, is it?' he asked, pretending to be offended. 'You must be those upper-class private-school girls I keep hearing about. The ones who are used to having servants. And never leave a tip.'

'Don't be a twink,' Niffy broke in, then introduced him to everyone round the table.

'I'm sorry . . . a twink? What is that exactly?' Dermot wanted to know. 'Is that special private-school speak?' He tapped the side of his nose.

'Yeah, we made it up in our dorm, during a midnight feast,' Amy teased, 'while we were in our long white nighties . . .'

'And night caps,' Niffy added. 'By candlelight.'

'This is just too exciting,' Dermot said, his elbows on their table as he looked ready to settle in for a cosy chat. 'But you're having me on. You're not really at boarding school, are you? In Edinburgh?'

He was looking at Gina as he asked this, so she nodded at him.

They weren't to find out what Dermot thought about this, because a loud voice called him back to work with the words: 'Oi, Dermot! Table nine!'

By 10.15p.m. Amy had to admit that Jason wasn't coming and it was time to get back to Mrs Knebworth before they were late. Min took her by the arm and led her out of the cafe with a face longer than a wet Sunday afternoon.

As the cab they'd hailed drove along Princes Street, Amy suddenly uttered a shriek. 'Look, over there! Stop the car!'

'What?' Min, Niffy and Gina all asked together as

the taxi sped on, the driver completely oblivious to his over-excited passenger.

'I saw him! I saw him walking along in the direction of the café!' Amy shouted, pushing down the window and craning her head out. 'We've got to turn back!'

'No we do not,' Min insisted. 'We're going to be late. It probably wasn't him anyway.'

'It was,' Amy said, a big smile across her face now. 'He was on his way. You see!' She sank back into her seat in bliss. 'He wanted to see me . . . he really did!'

'I think the Irish coffee was a mistake,' Niffy said, tapping the side of her head.

Chapter Eight

Now that school was into its third week, Gina was getting her written work back with marks and comments. It was obvious she wasn't doing very well. The only subject she was remotely good at was English: her English teacher, Mrs Parker, was enthusiastic about her work. But biology was hard, maths and physics were even harder, and her French homework had come back covered in lines, crosses and Madame Bensimon's neat handwriting: '*Appliquez-vous, appliquez-vous!*' Even Gina could work out what that meant: nothing to do with embroidery, but 'Try harder!'

Maybe she was never going to be allowed back home. Maybe her mother would make her languish here in Scotland for term after term.

History class was going to *kill* her. Was it possible to die of boredom? Gina, halfway through another lesson with Miss Ballantyne, was beginning to suspect that it was.

'Why are we copying notes from the board?' she'd hissed at Niffy.

'Because that is all we do in this class,' came the reply. '*Facts, girls! History is all about facts, not guesses, not surmises and certainly not opinions!*' Niffy imitated Miss Ballantyne in a high-pitched whisper.

Gina had gone on copying laboriously in longhand for a few more minutes, then she'd stuck her hand up in the air.

'Miss Ballantyne?'

'Yes?' The stern-faced teacher had turned from the board and peered at Gina over the top of her spectacles and the frilly blouse she wore buttoned up to the chin.

'Wouldn't it be possible for you to print out your notes and hand them out to us?' Gina asked.

She felt something of a collective intake of breath in the room at this question.

'These notes are not stored on a computer,' came the brisk reply. 'I can't just *print them out*!'

'Well, what about photocopying them?' Gina wasn't going to be fobbed off. 'It would save us all so much time.'

A gasp, both from Miss Ballantyne and Gina's class-mates, met this outrageous suggestion.

'Really!' Miss Ballantyne snapped, giving the icy look St Jude's staff had nearly all perfected.

'What?' Gina had asked.

'These notes are the fruit of years of teaching; they are covered with my edits, with my thoughts and observations. They are not just to be photocopied and handed out, erm . . .'

'Gina Peterson,' Gina had offered, then, cheekily referring to the teacher's age, she added, 'Maybe you knew my mother, Lorelei Winkelmann?'

Miss Ballantyne's face gave a distinct flash of recognition at the name and she looked at Gina closely. 'Indeed!' she snapped 'Well, we shall see how *you* fare, Gina.'

Gina would have liked to ask something about her mother, but Miss Ballantyne had turned back to the board and was writing again.

The conversation was clearly over and the boredom of the history lesson continued without any further outrageous interruptions.

'She wouldn't know what else to do with us,' Niffy whispered into Gina's ear. 'She makes every class copy out the same notes year after year. I've even checked a

Fifth Year's old jotters – exactly the same, word for word.'

Gina was hoping that at least the physics lesson would go a bit better, because she'd been receiving some intensive tuition from Min. Last night, in the study room, while Amy worked on a detailed sketch of Jason's face and Niffy busied herself drawing her horse, Ginger, over and over again, Min and Gina had tried to get to grips with the physics homework.

Gina had watched Min do solution after elegant solution. She'd listened, she'd copied, she'd hesitantly tried to do the examples herself as Min watched. Then she thought she'd finally got it.

Now, as Mr Perfect called her up to his desk, she wasn't so sure.

'Great homework,' he told her as he flicked through the pages she'd worked on with Min. 'Such a dramatic improvement. You're suddenly on a par with Asimina.'

Uh-oh. Gina thought she'd detected a worrying hint of playfulness in that comment.

'Would you talk me through this one please?' Mr Perfect asked, pointing at one of the pages of her homework.

Gina tried; well . . . she began, she stumbled on, she cleared her throat, she meandered . . . Everything Min had told her seemed to have evaporated from her head.

Finally, sensing the giggles rising from the class, not to mention the heat from Gina's cheeks, Mr Perfect told her to go and sit down, with the parting shot: 'I'm glad you're benefiting from some extra tuition at the boarding house, but I think it's best if everyone works at their own pace.'

He looked directly at Min as he said this, and there was no mistaking Penny Boswell-Hackett's mean snigger. Gina went back to her seat with her cheeks burning.

'Sorry,' Min whispered to her.

Gina blinked hard to contain the rising tears. Several seats along, there was another girl who was also trying not to cry. She was blowing her nose, wiping at her face with her tissue and sniffing hard. Gina remembered that her name was Jenny and wondered if any of her friends knew anything about her.

'Jenny Scott?' Amy asked when Gina met her in one of the corridors during the lunch break. 'She's all over the place – sneaking out to the loos to sob, coming back to class with a red face. I don't know what it is. Not even

Giselle, her best friend, knows. Hope it's something really juicy though – we haven't had a scandal for ages. Maybe she's pregnant!' Amy tried to look excited, but as they were talking about a girl who still wore two pigtails, woolly knee socks and shoes with buckles, this hardly seemed likely.

'Maybe someone's died,' Gina suggested.

'Maybe her cat,' said Amy unsympathetically.

'Oh look, it's the little boarding-house cheat. I wouldn't bother copying Amy's homework because she's not good at anything, are you, Amy?'

'Well, apart from spending Daddy's money,' added a second voice.

Neither Gina nor Amy needed to turn round to see who was behind these horrible remarks.

'Get knotted, Penny,' Amy snarled.

'Oh, I'm sorry, am I in your way? I'm just signing up for the Year Four debating contest. Is that why you're here too? Oh no, I forgot, you're not good at debating, are you? It's not the kind of thing *you'd* learn at home. They still use their fists to settle every argument in Glasgow, don't they?'

Penny scrawled her name on the notice and then, with Louisa in tow, disappeared off down the corridor.

Amy turned her attention to the sheet of paper

on the notice board, which Penny had just signed.

'*Debaters wanted*,' she read out. '*All girls interested in the Year Four debating contest planned for the end of term, please sign up before Friday*... Well' – Amy reached for the pen dangling from the board by a long string – 'let's see what the loathsome cow thinks about this.'

'Are you sure?' Gina asked as Amy wrote her name right underneath Penny's.

'Oh yes, I'm sure. How hard can it be to argue with a sour-faced snob you can't stand?'

'*You did what?!*' Niffy was appalled by Amy's debating contest news.

She, Amy, Gina and two other boarders were all cosily eating toast and drinking mugs of tea in the Year Four sitting room that evening. (Gina understood tea now: people in Britain had to drink it all the time to stay warm. The sun never shone here, and when it did, it was pallid and weak, just like the tea.) Min was half-heartedly playing the shabby-looking piano.

'Is there anything you're not good at?' Gina had asked as Min struck up.

'*Mais ... oui!*' Min had replied.

'Let me just get this straight: you've signed up with

Penny Boswell-Hackett for the Year Four debating competition? Are you out of your mind?' Niffy was so het up, she spluttered tea onto her chair. 'Balls,' she added, uselessly wiping at the stain with her hand.

'Well, how hard can it be?' Amy protested. 'You'll all help me to write a good speech. Anyway – Penny? She couldn't kick her own arse!'

'*How hard can it be?!*' Niffy's voice was raised. 'Amy! Hello! We're talking about Penny! Penny's entire family is made up of lawyers. Her dad's a judge, her uncle's a sheriff, her mum's a barrister, her big sister's at Edinburgh University doing – guess what – law! Penny was born to debate. She probably has to make the case for how her eggs are going to be cooked at breakfast every morning. Her parents will be coaching her. They'll want to see her wipe the floor with her opposition. You'll be demolished!'

Amy was not looking quite so confident now, and Min's piano playing had slowed so she could listen in to this.

'What's the topic?' Min wanted to know. 'What are you debating?'

'I don't know yet,' Amy answered. 'But you'll help me, won't you? Anyway, it's a home crowd – no one likes Penny. It'll be fine . . .' She looked from face to face, willing them to support her.

There was a pause long enough for Gina – who knew nothing about debating contests but could, according to Mrs Parker, write a decent essay – to feel that she had to step in with a bit of Californian 'can do' attitude. 'You're right,' she insisted. 'Someone has to stand up to that brat. We'll train you, Amy. We'll make sure you win.'

'Or at least don't look like a totally useless, utter tit,' Niffy added, without quite so much optimism.

Way after dark, way after lights out, Niffy and Amy sat on the wide top rung of the fire escape outside the dorm window, wrapped in their dressing gowns: Amy in pink silk with dainty matching slippers, Niffy in a bobbly blue tartan thing inherited from her brother. Her slippers, like many Nairn-Bassett household items, had embroidered crests, but far too many holes.

'What are you doing out there?' Min called to them more than once. 'You better not be smoking, or I'm going to tell the Neb, I really am. Haven't you heard of lung cancer? Heart attacks? Pulmonary obstructive disease? Emphysema?'

This just made Niffy and Amy giggle because they

were sharing a perfumed cigarette bought for 60p from a Year Four who kept her Silk Cut hidden in an empty bottle of baby powder.

From the fire escape they could see the Neb's bedroom window on the ground floor. The light clicked on behind pulled curtains and Amy breathed in sharply and tried to flatten herself against the railing.

'Don't worry,' Niffy said calmly. 'She can't see us.'

'How do you know?'

'I've seen her open the curtains and look out before, but she's not spotted me yet.'

'How often are you out here?' Amy asked.

'Oh . . . once in a while.'

Amy thought she could detect a tinge of sadness in these words. She didn't like to think of Niffy being out here on her own, worrying about something.

'Is everything OK with you?' she wondered.

'Yup, everything's fine.' Niffy let smoke puff out of her nostrils.

'Everything OK at home?'

'No!' Niffy gave a smoky laugh. 'It's never OK at home. You know perfectly well they're always fighting about money – how to make the hundreds of thousands needed to keep Blacklough from falling to bits. But meanwhile they phone, they email, they even send postcards telling me that everything's fine.' Making her voice even plummier, she added, 'That's the Nairn-Bassett way.'

'They should just sell that dump, buy somewhere much smaller, have a great stash in the bank and be happy,' Amy informed her.

'Ha! Haven't I explained it to you? Blacklough has been in my mother's family for five generations!'

'Oh, who cares!' Amy said pithily. 'We had rickets in my family for three generations. No one seems to miss them now they've gone!'

Niffy shot her a look which made it plain that family stately homes and malnutrition weren't exactly the same thing.

'They'll get over it,' Amy assured her.

There was silence while Niffy moodily smoked the cigarette down, then stubbed it out and momentarily wondered what to do with the butt before flicking it into the gutter.

Amy realized she could contain her secret no longer and burst out with the news: 'I got an email from Jason!'

'You didn't!' Niffy sounded almost too surprised.

'Oh yes I did! It said . . .' And Amy began to recite, word perfectly, because she had read the email at least thirty times over: '*Hi Amy, hope this is yr email address. Got it from someone's sister. Are you going to invite a few of us to the Year 4 ball next month then? All best, Harry, Milo, Peter and Jason.*'

'I'm not sure if that technically counts as an email from Jason,' Niffy pointed out.

But Amy, her arms wrapped tightly round her knees, wasn't listening. She just smiled very, very broadly at the dim, early summer night sky. 'He's going to come to the ball!' she said quietly. '*The summer ball!* It's just pure . . . dead . . . brilliant!'

But then, with a wail of panic, she added, 'What am I going to wear?'

Chapter Nine

What to wear to the ball? How to do your your hair for the ball? Which dances to practise for the ball? These questions took up a serious amount of the girls' free time during the following weeks.

Along with all the rumours and counter-rumours about which boys were coming and which were not:

'*Jason is definitely coming, he emailed!*'

'*Llewellyn won't be allowed! He's not at one of the invited schools.*'

'*Oh dear, what will Penny do?*'

'*Better watch out, Amy – it's happened before!*'

'*Angus has been asking Jason if you're definitely going to be there, Niff!*'

'*Has not!*'

'*Has.*'

The four inhabitants of Daffodil dorm, along with another two boarders from their year – Suzie and Lucy

– were once again in the Arts Café on a Saturday after-noon, exhausted after yet another trawl round all the potential dress shops in Edinburgh.

Amy still had '*nothing, zip, nada!*' to wear. The fact that her chest of drawers and the two large suitcases under her bed were crammed full of clothes didn't make the slightest difference. Now she was totally depressed because Lucy had found a dress and she still hadn't.

'OK, I'm seriously considering the blue one in Harvey Nichols,' she told them, 'but they have a new delivery of stock next week – so I might just hang on a little bit longer to see if there's anything better in that.'

Amy might have been only fifteen, but she was already on first-name terms with the personal shopper on floor two.

'What are you wearing again?' she asked Gina.

'A really nice pink dress. I bought it with my mom to bring over here and we got shoes for it too.'

'Oh!' came Amy's envious sigh. 'This is just mince. I really want to be sorted out. There's only one more Saturday to go!'

'Till what?' Dermot asked, arriving at their table with a tray of coffees. As the boarders were now café regulars, he was getting to know them quite well.

'None of your beeswax,' Suzie told him with a smile.

Gina jumped in to inform him, 'There's a dance at school, but over here it's apparently called a ball.'

'Ooooh! Are we all going to the ball, gerrrrls?' He rolled his 'r's theatrically. Then, spotting the large shopping bag tucked under Lucy's chair, he leaned down to take a peek inside, before throwing up his hands and declaring, '*Cerise chiffon . . . I am overcome! My dear*' – he gazed at Lucy – '*you are going to be the belle of the ball.*'

When he finished by wiping an imaginary tear from his eye, Niffy and Gina didn't just laugh, but also applauded his performance.

Dermot made a little bow then bounced off to take orders from another table.

'Isn't he a sweetheart?' Gina whispered.

'No wonder you lot are in here every weekend!' Suzie said. 'Who is he?'

'He's Dermot. His dad runs the café and he's just about to sit his Highers. But all the time he's not studying, he's in here earning his pocket money.' Gina, who had never even had to make her own bed to qualify for her generous allowance, found this deeply impressive.

'Niffy? What about you?' Amy was still on about dresses. 'Min's going to wear my little red number, but what are you planning?'

'Oh . . .' Niffy stretched out her long arms and yawned, as if this was the most boring conversation in the world. 'I thought I'd go to Topshop – they have dresses, don't they? Quite cheap? I've only got about thirty pounds left in my account.'

'Thirty quid?' Amy was truly horrified. 'You can't even get a decent eye shadow for that!'

'Well, I'll leave it just a little bit longer. Maybe my dad will stick a tenner in an envelope if I ask him nicely.'

'So what is this ball going to be like?' Gina asked, beginning to feel quite excited about it. 'Are the guys really going to come in tuxedos? Like in the movies?'

'Yeah, or kilts!' Niffy enthused. 'You can't really say you've experienced Scotland until you've had a twirl round the dance floor with a guy in a kilt.'

'Yeah, but you have to watch the metal buttons on kilt jackets when the twirling gets wild,' Amy added. 'They can cause flesh wounds.'

This didn't sound so cool to Gina. 'What!' she exclaimed. 'I wasn't going to get involved in any of your complicated Scottish dances anyway, but now I'm definitely propping up the bar.'

'Oh yes, there will be all the non-alcoholic fruit punch you can drink,' Suzie informed her.

'What am I going to wear?!' Amy wailed once again, her head in her hands.

Chapter Ten

'Are you going into town?' Niffy asked at breakfast on the actual day of the *actual* Year Four summer ball. Finally the long awaited event had arrived!

'Yeah, just as soon as we've finished,' Amy told her. 'They've had to do a few alterations, but my dress is going to be ready to collect just as soon as the doors open this morning.' There was no disguising the excitement in her voice. She had finally found it – the dream dress. The dress that would be the envy of every single girl at the ball.

'Well, it's just . . . I thought maybe I'd go in with you and you could help me look in Topshop, because I'm still not sorted out.'

Amy looked at Niffy in disbelief. 'What!' she exclaimed. 'It's today, Niffy. Tonight. You can't go in your jodhpurs, you know.'

'Shame really,' Niffy growled.

'I don't know if I've got time to help you look,' Amy said. 'Gina and I were going to go in, get the dress, buy some new lipsticks, then come back here and do our hair, our nails, our make-up . . . you know.'

'Amy, it's eight thirty-five a.m.,' Min reminded her.

'OK, here's the plan,' Niffy instructed. 'We set off after breakfast, you and Gina go to Harvey Nicks, I go to Topshop, then at twelve thirty we meet in the Arts Café. You have to be ready by then, Amy,' she warned. 'You have to have the new dress, the new shoes, the new blusher, new lip gloss, new hair gel and whatever else it is you need. Then we'll have a coffee to perk us all up and head back here with hours to spare before the seven-thirty start. What about you, Min? Are you coming with us?'

Min set down the large glass of orange juice she was drinking and answered, 'Amy's lending me something, so I'm fine. I've got to put in some training this morning. I'm so slow. Grinding to a standstill.'

Just then, Selina Davis, one of their fellow Year Four boarders, returned to the table, gingerly dangling two fresh pieces of toast in her fingernails, with the news: 'You do know that it's Daffodil's turn to wash up after breakfast today.'

The groan this brought from the four girls was so

loud and so heartfelt that the Neb scuttled over from her table at the dining-room window to find out what was wrong.

'We're on washing up!' Amy practically shrieked. 'I can't wash up – I've got to go out and get my dress! And think of our nails!' she pleaded. 'All the rubber gloves have holes in them. Our hands will get trashed. Couldn't we swap with whoever's on next week? One of the Year Three dorms? Pleeeeeeeease!'

'Oh dear.' Mrs Knebworth went over and looked at the rota taped neatly to the kitchen door. 'Now why did I not think of the Year Four ball when I was making that up? No ... two of next week's dishwashers are away home this weekend, so I can't help you there, I'm afraid.'

She turned round, and the expected look of sympathy came out looking very like a smirk; immediately, all four Daffodils were convinced she had done this on purpose.

'I'll wash,' Niffy volunteered. 'My hands are knackered anyway.' And she held out her rough hands with their short square nails and chewed cuticles for inspection.

'I've got really dark purple nail varnish – I'll smarten them up with that tonight,' Amy offered in response to this – in her opinion – selfless act of martyrdom.

* * *

The Arts Café was busy by 12.30. Almost every table was filled as Amy and Gina scoured the space for Niffy, sure that she would be here by now.

At first they didn't spot her, because they were looking at the smaller tables, expecting to find her on her own, but then Gina pointed to one of the packed sofa corners, where four scruffily dressed boys were laughing loudly at a story being told by an equally scruffy girl perched on the very edge of her seat: Niffy!

'Oh, hi!' she called, spotting them hovering, laden down with Harvey Nichols white and gold shopping bags. 'Over here! Finn will get you coffees. How did I manage to forget that my brother has a weekend out and said he would be in Edinburgh?' she added, and smacked at her forehead with her hand. 'Duh!'

'Craigiefield boys,' Amy quietly explained to Gina. 'It's a really posh boarding school for boys in the middle of nowhere. They only get let out once in a while, and Niffy's brother, Finn, is one of them.'

'Amy! You know everyone. Gina meet Finn, Euan and Jamie from Craigiefield and their friend Charlie from St Lennox's,' was Niffy's casual introduction. 'And show, show!' she insisted, pointing at their bags.

'No!' Amy said firmly. 'Not here. It's a surprise. What about you? Any luck?'

'Yes!' Niffy reached down and fished around for her plastic bag. From inside she hoicked out a strapless, electric-blue taffeta mini-dress with a flared skirt and net petticoat. 'Not bad, eh?' She grinned. 'Reduced to fifteen pounds.'

'Really?' Amy tried to sound enthusiastic.

'Yeah, it's a size sixteen – might need a safety pin or two – but a bargain!'

The boys were grinning and making approving noises.

'Great colour!'

'Great length!'

'All girls should have to wear dresses like that.'

'Yeah. It should be the law.'

Finn stood up, revealing a physique as long and gangly as his sister's. Like the other three boys, he was draped in a mac, baggy jeans, several scarves and overgrown hair, which had to be regularly swept back from his face.

But despite the scruffiness, these were rich boys. They were tall, with healthy good looks, and Gina could see the expensive watches, the smart shoes, the discreet labels. Plus, she was beginning to understand that not everyone in Scotland spoke like these boys did, as if they were distantly related to the Queen.

'What would you like to drink, girls?' Finn asked.

'Sit down, man, there's a waiter.' Jamie pointed to Dermot, who came over, skinny as ever and still dressed in the see-through white shirt.

'Hello, dorm girls.' He greeted them with only a brief smile: clearly the presence of the boys was putting him off.

Amy and Gina, both now squeezed between Euan and Charlie on one of the leather sofas, ordered Cokes.

As Gina took off her jacket and pushed it behind her, Charlie, a beefy blond guy who already looked about thirty-five, leaned in just a little too close.

'Lovely to meet you,' he schmoozed. 'Now, I'm coming to a ball at your school tonight, but what about inviting my friends along as well?'

The fingertips of the hand resting on his knee were brushing ever so lightly past Gina's leg. Why, in every group of boys, was there always one lech? And why had she been landed with him?

'Yeah, I've told them about tonight's thing at school,' Niffy explained, 'and I'm sure if they dressed up, no one would notice. I mean, it's not like there's a ticket check at the door or anything.'

Amy didn't look so sure, but Finn seemed very enthusiastic. 'Yeah, fantastic. We're staying at Charlie's for the weekend. His people have got a big place in the New Town.'

By now, Gina had learned that 'people' meant parents and 'big place in the New Town' tended to indicate a five-storey Georgian townhouse, Grade A listed, Scottish Heritage registered, price tag about £2 million.

'We'll borrow some clothes,' Finn went on, 'and turn up at seven thirty for some fun.'

Borrow some clothes? Amy just about choked. After all the trouble she'd taken to find the right dress! After all the trouble she was planning to go to: straightening her hair, applying her evening make-up, shaving, manicuring, plucking, and she would be dancing with cretins like this, who would show up, probably drunk, in clothes they had *borrowed*!

Surely Jason wasn't going to be like this? When Amy thought of Jason at the dance, she imagined him in a dark, perfectly cut dinner suit, with a white silk scarf and a carefully knotted bow tie. He would ask her to dance; they would skim through a waltz, then maybe he would get her a drink (school non-alcoholic punch, sadly – no bubbles of champagne frothing in crystal flutes between them).

Amy, would you like to come outside, get a breath of fresh air? he would ask, and she'd shiver from head to toe because everybody knew what 'would you like to come outside' meant.

Just the thought of kissing him made her stomach flip and her toes curl. He'd ask her permission, of course. In his smooth and chocolaty voice, he'd utter words like: *Amy, I'd really like to kiss you . . . do you think that would be OK?*

And before she could even breathe, their lips would touch and his beautiful cheeks and silky dark hair would be right against her face, his arms pulling her towards him. It would be sooooo romantic. Nothing like the other kisses she'd experienced to date. She was sure, absolutely certain, that Jason was the one: he was going to be her first love.

'Tomorrow – yeah, we'd love to, wouldn't we?' Niffy's nudge brought Amy out of her daydream.

'What?' Amy asked, wondering what Niffy had agreed to now.

'Go round to Charlie's for afternoon tea?'

'Fantastic.' Charlie seemed to be breathing right into Gina's ear now.

Dermot arrived with their coffees and banged them moodily down on the table.

'Hi, Dermot,' Amy ventured. 'How are you doing?'

'Oh, fine,' he said, but with a heavy note of sarcasm. 'Having a ball, are we? And these are your dashing partners, I suppose?'

'Dermot!' Gina leaned back in her chair and turned round to face him. 'What's the matter?'

'Nothing,' he replied, but she could see from his expression that this wasn't true.

'D'you want to come?' she asked suddenly, wanting to make him feel better. 'I mean, if we can sneak these guys in without a proper invitation, I'm sure we could get you in too.'

Dermot was smiling at her now. 'That's a very kind offer,' he told her. 'I've never been to a ball before.'

'Neither have I,' she said.

His eyes held hers. 'I can't do country dancing.'

'Neither can I! Come on, it'll be fun.'

He ran his hand through his hair and laughed. 'No, I can't.'

'Why not?'

'Too many reasons, Gina! Too many reasons!' he told her. 'Number one, I'd stick out like a sore thumb; number two, I'm working here till eleven p.m.; number three, funnily enough I don't just happen to have a dinner jacket hanging in the back of my cupboard right now – it's at the cleaner's!' he joked and gave her a wink.

Charlie inched his wallet out of his back pocket and peeled a tenner from inside. 'Hey, waiter! I'll take care of these,' he boomed. 'Anyone for anything else?'

Dermot smiled at Gina to signal the end of their little chat, then reached over to take the money from Charlie's hand. He turned on his heel and headed off, forgetting to wait for any further orders.

'That was a bit bloody rude,' Charlie commented, loud enough for Dermot to hear.

'Shhh!' Gina insisted. 'It's packed in here – he's probably just really, really busy.'

'Oh, I forgot – Yank at the table: suck up to the staff, everyone!' Charlie sneered.

By 6.50, the atmosphere on Year Four's floor of the boarding house was close to hysterical. Eighteen girls were rushing about in various stages of dress and undress, screaming for hairdryer sockets, quick-drying nail polish, make-up corrector wipes and lost lipsticks.

Zips were jamming, hair was misbehaving, mascara was smudging . . . it was pre-party pandemonium. In just forty minutes, the summer ball, the social highlight of the whole term, would begin.

A girl called Jo was in tears because a glass of water had just been spilled on her satin dress. Selina's freshly highlighted hair was deemed to still 'stink of bleach' even though she'd washed and dried it twice. A friend was spraying expensive perfume into the offending locks.

In Daffodil dorm there had been frenzied activity, but now something approaching calm was descending. Min looked sweet: she'd borrowed a bright-red, knee-length, strapless silk dress from Amy which glowed against her black hair and freshly moisturized brown skin. Amy wasn't mad about Min's choice of sensible black patent pumps, but Min had ruled out squeezing her feet into the heel-crushing red shoes again.

Gina was in baby pink, a slinky little cocktail number, her shoes the kind of baby-pink suede confections that made Amy gasp in admiration.

'Isn't your dress a bit tight for dancing?' she had already warned.

To which Gina had replied, 'Like I care! I can't do a single one of your crazy Scottish numbers anyway.'

'You have to dance!' Amy had insisted. 'What's the point of going to a ball if you don't dance? That's the best bit!'

And suddenly, at the thought of holding Jason's hand and feeling his arm at her back as they spun round the dance floor, Amy had felt almost sick with nerves. What if he didn't ask her? She wouldn't be able to bear it. What if he *did* ask her? She wouldn't be able to bear it!

She stood in front of the mirror one last time, turning her shoulders side on and looking for any detail she might have missed. But there was already no doubt which of all the Year Four girls had the best dress.

After phoning her father from the personal shopping suite in Harvey Nichols and begging him to approve an immediate extension on her credit card limit, Amy had bagged the ballgown of her dreams. The ballgown of any girl's dreams.

With a draped bodice of creamy chiffon and a wide skirt, ballerina length, trimmed with (wait for it) *feathers* – actual real, snowy, fluffy feathers – this was a dress made in heaven. It had certainly come with a price tag that was out of this world.

'*Are you sure? Are you really, really sure about this?*' Gina had double-checked with her friend as they had looked once again at the four-figure bill. Amy had just nodded and handed over the plastic.

Now, with her pale hair piled up loosely, light

make-up and the shimmer from understated drop pearl earrings, Amy looked sensational. Of course she was going to be the most beautiful girl at the ball. A dress like that had authority. It said: *Pay attention – I am the most precious jewel here in the most exquisite setting.*

'It's just wonderful,' Min said, coming up to stroke Amy's skirt. 'But aren't you worried it might get spoiled? What if someone spills coffee on it?'

'No chance!' Amy assured her. 'This is a work of art. Even people like Penny will respect that and stand back.'

'Oh, fluffy bum! I've ripped my tights! Does anyone have spares?'

Niffy's question brought an exasperated sigh from Amy. 'Yes, but hurry up, we have to go! We'll have to wear our day shoes, walk over to the school block and then change there. So unbelievably inconvenient!'

Niffy struggled to get her long legs into the new pair of tights.

'Don't pull so hard!' Amy warned her. 'You'll rip those ones too.'

'But they're not long enough,' Niffy complained, 'and this dress is so short, I'm going to have my gusset hanging down!'

She stood up. Despite Amy's best efforts with her hair and nails and Min's diligent pinning of her bodice, the effect wasn't great.

Niffy looked like a messy, schoolgirl version of a bunny girl. The dress was so short and her legs were so indecently long.

'Well?' She held out her arms and attempted a curtsey. 'What do you think?'

'It's really nice,' Gina assured her.

'Funky, huh?' Niffy asked. 'Are we set? Shall we go?'

'Shoes,' Min pointed out. 'You need to put on your shoes.'

'Shoes?' This seemed to confuse Niffy. 'Shoes!' she repeated.

'Yes, your *shoes*,' Amy said, as if speaking to a naughty toddler.

'I haven't got any shoes,' Niffy revealed. 'I didn't think about shoes.'

'Oh, for God's sake, Nif!' Amy's patience was well and truly exhausted now. 'What do you mean you didn't think of shoes? Everyone thinks of shoes! Everyone who buys a dress works out which shoes to wear with it. What are you? Fashion retarded? No one has feet as big as yours! What the bloody hell are you going to do?'

* * *

By the time the boarders arrived in the school hall, many of the day girls were already there doing double takes, hardly recognizing each other at first glance now that they were out of uniform and in full-on glamour mode.

Niffy's outfit drew plenty of friendly comment. The strange thing was, as soon as she'd strapped on the clumpy but clean tall riding boots with buckles, the mini-dress seemed to work much better. Maybe she'd just relaxed into it, now that she was wearing her favourite boots. Because Nif was as tall and thin as a rail with fabulous rider's posture, it didn't matter that she had a big nose, horsy face and cheap dress; tonight she looked like a catwalk model in some mad designer's latest brainwave.

But she wasn't drawing gasps in quite the same way that Amy was: gasps of admiration from friends; gasps of envy from others.

In that dress, Amy didn't stand a chance of escaping the inevitable showdown with Penny and friends. In fact, Penny, in a floaty floral green number, was already circling.

'It's a dance, Amy, not a performance of *Swan Lake*,' was Penny's starter for ten.

'Yeah, so I heard.' Amy turned away, hoping to escape any further remarks.

But Penny went on, 'Daddy bought you the wrong thing then, did he? But then he's probably never been to a ball at a proper school, has he?'

Amy looked back over her shoulder at Penny, whose pretty face was spoiled by the sneer spread across it. Why couldn't she just leave Amy alone? At least for tonight. This was a big hall – there was plenty of room for them to avoid each other.

'Yeah, Penny,' Amy began, not able to walk away from the insult, 'I suppose that's why Llewellyn isn't here tonight – because he's not at a proper school either. You know, I'm just sooo sad that my dad is loaded and can buy me whatever I want. I mean, it's not exactly tragic, is it? The only thing here that's tragic is the dress that you're wearing.'

With that, Amy let her dainty white and silver shoes carry her away to the other side of the room as quickly as possible.

Fortunately, this was the moment when the first busload of boys was decanted at the school. Troupes of them – in tweedy kilt jackets and multi-coloured kilts or sleek black dinner jackets with bow ties coolly askew – thronged into the hall with their tousled hair and goofy grins. They looked just slightly older and slightly wilder than the roomful of girls, who all seemed to pause for a moment . . . make a collective gasp, then start up again with the buzz of chat at a much higher level of excitement. There were frantically self-conscious conversations going on all round the room, as everyone pretended not to notice The Boys. But cheeks were flushing and hearts were skipping nervously as deep voices and testosterone started to flood the room.

'Niffy! There you are!' The group of gatecrashers, including Finn, headed over. Niffy, Gina and Min were relieved to have familiar males to talk to so soon, instead of having to stand about waiting for the ice to be broken. Amy gave a warm hello, but couldn't help scanning the room beyond them for any sign of Jason.

The ceilidh band began to play and everyone noticed, then pretended not to notice, prompting nervous boys to ask the girl standing closest to them to dance. Hardly anyone ever plucked up the courage to ask the girl with whom they really wanted to dance.

On the dance floor, it was tense, anxious, sweaty-palm central.

At least there was a formality to Scottish country dances – complicated steps to concentrate on instead of how to prolong or avoid eye contact. Little bursts of stilted conversation came between the different steps:

'So which school are you at?' Min was asking her partner.

'Oh, do you know Johnnie as well?' the boy dancing with Amy wanted to know.

'You got in then? What a blast!' Niffy said, swooping across the dance floor with her brother. 'Bum,' she cursed. 'This dance is much more complicated than I thought.' Then she trod firmly on someone's toe.

'*Ouch!*'

Gina had been whisked into Charlie's arms for an Eightsome Reel despite her protests that she couldn't dance. He was twirling her too hard and pushing her around. He seemed to take it as a personal insult that she didn't know the required steps, when everyone else around them seemed to be dancing so effortlessly.

'Could you just stop it?' she asked firmly when she'd been spun round roughly and then pulled back into line again. 'You're going to rip my dress.'

'Here's hoping,' he replied.

When the music finished, she abruptly turned away and went in search of a glass of regulation school punch and some moral support from friends.

'Having fun?' Niffy asked, heading back to the dance floor, a boy on each arm. Maybe she was bringing a spare. 'Dashing White Sergeant,' she explained. 'It's a three-way!'

Niffy was a hilariously oblivious boy magnet, it suddenly occurred to Gina. Every male within radius drooled, especially at the legs under the mini-dress, but she treated them all with casual affection, like big brothers . . . or, more likely, big dogs. Niffy had recently confessed to Gina that it had been months since she'd even thought of having a crush on anyone.

'Aha, you'll do.' A boy walked quickly up to Gina, holding out his hand in greeting. 'Jason Hernandez,' he announced. 'Can't remember if we've met or not, but would you like the next dance?'

Amy's Jason! Gina felt scared. Even one little dance with this guy was going to mean trouble with Amy. But, boy, was he handsome. It was the way he fixed his gaze on you, as if you were suddenly the only person in the room that mattered.

'Oh . . . I don't know any of these dances,' she told him. 'I'm kind of an embarrassing partner. I'm sure there are lots of other girls who'd be much better.' And she scanned about, somehow hoping to conjure Amy up before them.

But Jason, dark brown eyes firmly on hers, assured her, 'This is a waltz: everyone knows to waltz.'

'No! Not me. I'm from the States, remember? We invented disco.'

'Look, it's easy. How about I waltz and you just hold on tight, OK?'

He slipped his hand into hers; it wasn't exactly easy to refuse.

'So what's your name?' he asked.

'Gina Peterson,' she told him, way, way too conscious of her hand, which was now firmly in his grip.

'I remember you.' His face brightened. 'We met at the Filmhouse – you were looking for your friend's contact lens. Come on then, let's boogie.'

He didn't let go of her hand, just tucked her arm under his and led her out onto the dance floor.

She'd never waltzed before. In California, dancing with boys had meant doing her practised disco moves alongside the weird flapping and jiggling boys seemed to think would pass for steps. Even if Californian boys *did* waltz, she doubted it would be like this. Jason held her right hand up with his, then put his other hand easily across her bare back, and they whirled about the room with as much grace as a novice waltzer could muster. All the time, he didn't take his eyes from hers and continued to chat with the assurance of a sixteen-year-old Matt Damon.

Gina found she couldn't take her gaze from him either, which was probably just as well – otherwise she'd have seen the blizzard of snowy feathers spinning deliberately towards them from the other side of the dance floor.

Amy was steering her partner closer and closer towards Gina and Jason so she could keep her steely blue eyes trained on them at all times.

As soon as the music stopped, she managed to position herself right beside them, so that saying as confidently as possible, 'Hi, Jason! How are you?' was absolutely natural and unavoidable.

'Amy, hi! What an amazing dress!' he told her straight away. 'Harvey Nichols! I saw it in the window, but it looks much better on you.'

Wow! What an opening line! Amy wanted to burst with excitement. And he *was* wearing the black dinner suit with white silk scarf and fringing that she had imagined in her daydreams.

'Gina, you know Pete, don't you?' Amy introduced her waltzing partner. 'God, I'm so thirsty now. Would you be a doll and get us some drinks?'

Gina understood what she was to do perfectly: 'C'mon, Pete' – she smiled at the guy she remembered from the bookshop café – 'I'll need a spare pair of hands.'

She resisted the temptation to wink at Amy, who was now left all alone with Mr Dreamboat.

When Gina and Pete returned with the glasses of ruby punch, Amy and Jason had already gone. There they were on the dance floor together, Jason with his magnetic gaze now fixed firmly on Amy; Amy gazing back in a living daydream of happiness.

Gina couldn't help watching them. They made a very attractive couple, Amy so pale and blonde and stunningly dressed, Jason so dark and dapper. It was a fast, complicated dance, with marching, side kicks, spinning and bursts of the sort of bouncy waltz Gina thought might be a polka, but neither of them seemed to miss a step. The music was speeding up and they were both laughing and dancing faster and faster – until, with a loud final chord, the music stopped and Gina saw Amy slide her arm though Jason's. His face bent towards hers and they exchanged smiles and words, then she tossed her pretty head like a show pony, and led him coolly right out of the hall – though not without shooting an unmistakable victory grin at Gina.

When Pete offered himself as a dancing partner, Gina turned him down politely and said she had to head to the 'restrooms'. When he looked confused at this, she explained, 'I mean . . . loos? Bogs? The ladies?'

'Got you,' he replied with a wink.

Well, OK, yes, she wasn't exactly desperate to go, she was just curious to know if Amy was finally going to snag her man. Keeping close to the walls and door-ways for cover, Gina followed in the direction of Mr Dreamboat and Miss Featherpuff. She crept past the door of a darkened classroom but, through the window, a movement inside caught her attention.

'What's the matter?' Charlie was asking Min. 'I'm just trying to talk to you. Nothing wrong with that, is there?'

Min had come to Charlie's attention when she'd spun merrily in front of him on the dance floor. *Now*, he'd thought to himself, *there is a girl who knows how to have fun and who looks sensational in a red dress.* He'd steered her to the juice table, flirted with her and enjoyed her shy giggles in response. Yes, he'd thought, since the Californian girl was being so frosty, this one in the red dress would do instead.

'What about a little tour?' he'd asked, voice conspiratorially low.

'Of what?' Min had wondered.

'Your school, of course! Every male wants to know

what really goes on behind the doors of St Jude's . . . C'mon,' he'd wheedled when Min didn't look at all certain, 'we'll just stroll round some of the places on the ground floor – none of those old girls are going to care.' He'd directed her gaze to the table where the five members of the St Jude's staff in charge of tonight's event were deep in conversation with a handsome teacher from St Lennox's.

Charlie had taken her hand as they'd strolled together, and the frisson of holding hands with a boy as she walked along the school corridors had made Min almost breathless.

'How about this classroom?' Charlie had asked, leaning against the handle and pushing the door open.

Min had started to say, 'No! We can't go in there—' when she'd found herself being pulled in and the door firmly shut behind her. Immediately she was pinned against Charlie's beefy chest by Charlie's beefy arms.

'What are you doing?' she'd demanded to know.

'What's the matter? I'm just trying to talk to you – nothing wrong with that, is there?' Charlie had replied.

Min could smell his breath: it was beer – or maybe whisky-laced – he'd had something a lot stronger than the St Jude's punch, that was for sure. 'This isn't talking, this is mauling!' she'd insisted, feeling the pressure on her chest as Charlie squeezed her more tightly.

'Just a kiss!' he'd insisted. 'Try it – you might like it.' And he'd pushed his face with its boozy breath down towards hers.

'*No!*' she cried, and turned her face sideways so that he made contact with her ear. But this didn't deter him: he began to lick first her ear and then her neck.

'No, get off!' Min called out again, pulling away from the sloppy tongue working its way towards her shoulder. She kicked him sharply in the shin, but he just giggled.

What happened next surprised Min almost as much as it did Charlie. The classroom door flew open, walloping Charlie so hard on the back of the head that he let go of Min and yelped in pain.

Gina appeared, grabbed Min by the hand and pulled her out of the room with the words: 'In the States we have laws against that kind of thing, you creep! Leave now. Right now, or we'll have you thrown out.'

Amy's bare arm and shoulders were goose-pimpling – and not just because of the cool breeze ruffling the pale June evening outside. Jason's arm was wound round hers and they were strolling through the school grounds, not exactly saying much, but then Amy wasn't sure if she would be heard above the sound of her heart thumping.

'Where are you taking me then?' Jason wanted to know.

'Oh . . . erm . . . well, nowhere in particular,' Amy told him.

'Not some special quiet corner then?' he asked, looking at her with a smile she thought was just slightly sly.

'Well . . . I . . . erm . . .' she stumbled, no idea what to say next. Usually she was so cool and together with boys. Jason just had this strange effect on her.

'Aren't you thinking about kissing?' Jason asked. 'Because if you are, we could stop and do it right here.'

Here was fine, she told herself over the now manic drumming in her chest. There was a sliver of pale moon in the sky; there were cherry trees in the background *shhhhhshhhh*ing in the wind. So now he was going to catch her up in his arms and give her the amazing kiss she'd been waiting for.

He turned, drew in close . . . She closed her eyes and tipped her face, and then his lips were pushed down against hers. Their front teeth clashed together and, in surprise at this, she pulled back slightly. That's when she heard the catcalls and the applause.

'Waaaaaaay-haaaaaay!'

'Racy Jasey scores again!'

'Fast work, man. Fast work!'

'Don't worry about that,' Jason insisted, pulling her in for a second kiss.

But Amy turned and saw that on one of the benches, not even ten metres away from them, three St Lennox boys were parked, sharing a cigarette and a can of beer.

'C'mon,' Amy insisted, wanting to get him away from these spectators so they could have a second, hopefully more successful attempt at the kiss.

'Oh . . . I'll just say a quick hello,' Jason replied, disentangling his arm from hers and heading, to her astonishment, towards the boys on the bench.

'Introduce us to your new girlfriend!' one of them insisted.

But Amy had already turned on her heel and began to run back towards the school.

Min was also walking round the building. She'd thanked Gina but then shrugged her off and headed outside. To cool down, she'd told herself, but really she wanted to shed the few tears that she knew were about to escape in private. She felt so silly, so furious with herself. Such a foolish situation to get into. And of course she'd over-reacted. Why hadn't she just told Charlie *playfully* to get lost? Or why hadn't she just kissed him? Would that have been so bad? She felt so naïve! Gina had known just how to handle Charlie. Why hadn't she been able to do that?

It was because she knew absolutely nothing about boys that she always seemed to get the idiot bloke . . . and ended up feeling like an idiot herself.

'Min? What are you doing out here?' Amy spotted her just as she was wiping the tears from her cheeks. 'Hey, what's the matter?'

Once Min had explained as briefly as she could, Amy's consolation was a frank: 'Well, I feel like a total numpty too. And I *wanted* him to kiss me.'

As they walked round the corner of the building together, they heard distant but definite whoops coming from a far corner of the playing fields.

Peering out over the playing fields, they could make out four figures, all carrying bottles and glowing cigarette ends, who appeared to be holding races on the running track.

Two of the figures looked as if they were wearing kilts; one was in a dinner suit – they could see the shirt glowing white. One was definitely a girl in a very short mini-dress and a pair of clumpy boots.

'Niffy?' Min wondered.

'No doubt,' Amy agreed.

So they set off down the path at the edge of the field to rescue her . . . from herself.

As they got closer, Niffy and the other racers lined up. First they took deep swigs from their bottles, then, with a whoop from Niffy, they set off across the field. For fifty metres or so, one of the boys was out in front, but as they reached their agreed finishing line, Niffy surged forward, dipping towards the imaginary tape like a pro. As she crossed, she whooped once again and flung her arms up into the air.

Unfortunately the mini-dress didn't follow and Niffy's bare boobs were suddenly right out there on display, as if they'd popped up to say hello.

Despite two of the boys collapsing to the grass, helpless with laughter, Niffy didn't register. It was her brother, Finn, the third boy, who drew her attention to the situation with the words: 'Tit alert, Lu! Tit alert!'

When Niffy looked down to see that the mini-dress bodice had plummeted, she didn't cross her arms or scream; she assessed the situation with astonishing calmness, then got hold of the dress and matter-of-factly pulled it back up again.

'Whoops!' was all she said.

'Niffy!' Min caught up with her first. 'What are you doing out here?'

'Min!' Niffy looked very happy to see her. 'Could you pin me back in again? Something seems to have come undone.'

'Yeah, of course,' Min said and began work on Niffy's bodice.

Amy, still upset about Jason, found herself ticking the boys off for bringing in wine and cigarettes.

'If someone finds us out here with this stuff, we could all get expelled!' she hissed. 'We need to get back into the building! And what about the bottles?' she asked when one of the boys started walking back across the playing field with a wine bottle dangling from one hand, a fag still lit in the other. 'You can't take them with you! Where are you going to put them?'

One of the kilted guys just laughed, drained his bottle and flung it at the hedge bordering the playing field.

'Don't do that! You tosser!' Amy said, surprised at how sharp it sounded – well, she had already been feeling rattled, but the heel of her white and silver suede shoe had just sunk deep into the earth, and now she was furious.

'OK, miss!' came the cheeky reply.

'Sorry.' Finn walked towards her and began apologizing for them all. 'Sorry to get you all the way out here – you should have left us to it.'

'I didn't know who Niffy was with,' Amy explained. 'We all look out for each other.'

'That's very kind,' Finn told her.

With Niffy still in Min's safe hands, Amy and Finn began to walk slowly towards the school building.

When Min had finished pinning the bodice, Niffy took a few more long swigs from the bottle of white wine in her hand, then drew on the remaining stub of cigarette.

'What are you doing?' Min scolded. 'Put the bottle down and put that out. Now!' She pointed to the cigarette in horror. 'If anyone catches you, you'll get expelled straight away, no questions asked.'

'Ha!' Niffy simply put the cigarette between her lips and took another long drag.

'Oh, that's what you want, is it?' Min asked sarcastically.

'Maybe,' Niffy said, almost harshly.

Then, to Min's surprise, Niffy squatted down, tucking her dress in behind her boots, and burst into tears.

'Don't you cry as well.' Min crouched down beside her. 'That will make three of us – three bawling at the summer ball. Maybe they've put something in the punch. What's the matter?'

When Niffy just pressed the heels of her hands hard against her eyeballs, Min said soothingly, 'Maybe it's the wine. Maybe you've had too much. None of us exactly ate a proper supper.'

'Min' – Niffy took her hands away from her face – 'sometimes I think I should be living at home. You know, like normal people do. Sometimes I think it would be better for my mum and dad if I was at home. I'd stop them arguing so much.'

Min thought about her crowded, noisy family home where there was always something to do or someone to look after. In truth, she quite liked the peace and quiet of the boarding house, especially the study room, when no one else was about.

'My mother told me I would be at this school for just a few years, but I'll have my family for the whole of my life,' Min said, rubbing Niffy's shoulders. 'Why don't you think of it like that? And you know, if your parents have got problems, they need to sort them out themselves. There's probably nothing you can do for them.'

Then they heard a distant giggle and looked across the field to the illuminated path between the school building and the tennis courts, where a girl in a flowing green dress was walking hand in hand with a tall boy.

'Isn't that Penny?' Niffy asked in surprise.

'Oh no!' Min was horrified: there was no mistaking Penny's ravishing escort. 'She's with *Jason*!'

Chapter Eleven

When the ball finally came to an end on the stroke of midnight, with boys crowding onto buses, day girls being picked up by weary parents and boarders changing into flat shoes for the chilly walk back, there was no chance of everyone going straight to bed.

Most of the Year Four girls took mugs of tea and plates of toast to their sitting room, where they'd kicked off their shoes, loosened their pinching zips and exchanged all the gossip about the evening they'd just had.

Niffy, still giggly from the wine, flopped onto the sofa. She'd given up caring about her loose bodice and sagging gusset some time ago.

'Are you drunk?!' Selina wanted to know.

'Oh . . . just a glug or two,' Niffy replied.

'Keep well back from Mrs K,' Suzie warned. 'She's been leaning all over us trying to do a breathalyzer test.'

'And where did you get to,' Lucy asked Amy, 'with that very handsome boy?'

'Nothing happened,' Amy insisted. 'He just wanted to see the tennis courts.'

Everyone who heard this collapsed into giggles.

'Didn't I see him with—?' Janey, who happened to be sitting next to Min, was cut off by a sharp dig in the ribs.

'Who?' Amy insisted.

'And what about Angus?' Niffy asked, hoping the prank of the night would make everyone forget about where Jason had been and what he might or might not have been up to. 'I can't believe I missed that!' she went on. 'So what *exactly* happened?'

It was Selina who filled Niffy in with the details, while everyone else listened in.

'This big posh guy . . . Charlie something?' Selina hesitated.

'Fotheringham,' Niffy prompted her. 'I know him.'

'Right, well . . . Charlie was being teased by Angus about something – I don't know what it was, I didn't hear that bit—'

'Wasn't it something to do with Min?' Janey broke in.

'*No!*' Min insisted. She didn't want anyone else to know about her horrible, embarrassing minutes with Charlie.

'Will you just let Selina get on with this?' Niffy insisted.

Min turned her attention to her toast and began to spread Marmite thickly on top of the melting butter.

'Gross!' Gina whispered: her one mouthful of the stuff had convinced her that everyone who ate it must be mad.

'OK, Angus was teasing Charlie, Charlie started teasing Angus – something about he wasn't a real Scotsman – the usual!' Selina rolled her eyes, making her audience laugh – apart from Gina, who looked puzzled.

'You're only *a real Scotsman* if you don't wear anything under your kilt,' Lucy explained for her benefit, 'apparently.'

'Really?' Gina looked horrified now. 'No wonder so many guys came in tuxedos.'

'So then?' Niffy reminded Selina.

'Yeah, so then Angus clears his throat and announces to the entire hall: "Ladies and gentlemen, I give you a real Scotsman . . ." and he lifts his kilt right up and twirls around!'

'And . . .?' Niffy asked.

'He's wearing a leopard-print g-string!'

Everyone listening to this story exploded into laughter.

'Oh my Lord!' was Niffy's reaction. 'He must have done it for a bet! He told me he had something planned for later. Hairy bum?' she wanted to know.

'No! Smooth and quite muscley.'

This brought fresh peals of laughter.

Selina went on, 'Just about everybody in the room must have seen him, so Mrs Redpath and one of the St Lennox teachers took him by the arms and escorted him very politely out of the building.'

'Oh dear. I wonder what happened to him then . . .' Niffy said.

Janey finished the tale: 'He had to sit and wait on the school bus. I saw him when I went out for a little walk with Pete—'

'Ooooooh,' came the chorus back at her.

'And that's when I saw Amy's guy,' Janey went on smugly, 'walking down to the tennis courts with Penny Boswell-Hackett.'

Later, Amy undressed in the dorm in total silence.

NEW GIRL

When she left the room to wash her face and brush her teeth, Niffy told Min and Gina, 'That Janey is a right cow.'

Chapter Twelve

'God I can't bear this any longer!' Niffy groaned quietly. 'Make them stop, make it stop . . . I'm going to have to tell Madame it's not working: she's going to have to stop this. This is murder, a massacre. One of my favourite books!' she added, outraged. 'Why do we have to read it aloud round the class?'

'Because we haven't read enough on our own and Madame's in a strop with us,' Gina reminded her in a whisper.

Any casual observer of the Year Four French lesson would no longer have been able to pick out Gina as the newbie. Much to her relief, she no longer stuck out or felt quite so squeakily new. It wasn't just the short school skirt and tight cardigan Gina now wore to look just like the other girls; nor the narrow metal hair band, over-the-knee socks or Dolcis ballet pumps. No, it was more to do with knowing which desk to sit at in each classroom and which girls she knew would welcome her; knowing what they would be talking about and being up on all the latest gossip.

Thanks to Madame's strop, everyone was taking it in turn to read aloud two pages of the book they were studying: Alphonse Daudet's *Lettres de Mon Moulin*.

The monotonous voice of Claire, who was coming to the end of her two-page shift, rose slightly as she stumbled over her final words.

'What's the matter with Min?' Amy wondered.

The three of them looked over to the other side of the room, where Min's head was buried in her hands. Her book wasn't even open – that's how little attention she was paying to this lesson.

'Girls, stop it!' Madame snapped at them immediately. 'No chit-chatting in the corner. Luella!'

'But Madame Bensimon, I've read this book already,' Niffy objected.

'*All* of it?' Madame seemed slightly offended that one of her pupils should have raced ahead on her own like this. 'In French?'

'Yeah, three times,' Niffy confirmed.

Madame gave a 'Hmph' of discontent. 'Well then, I'll expect your reading to be word-perfect.'

Gina suspected Min's mood might have something

to do with what had happened in biology earlier. 'The teacher wanted to see her after class,' she whispered to Amy. 'She ran out of the room during an experiment.'

'It can't be that serious, can it?' Amy whispered back. But all three suspected, from the look on Min's face, that it was.

Min wasn't listening to anything going on in the French class. She was replaying the words of Mrs MacDuff, the biology teacher, in her mind.

She'd been summoned for 'a word' at the end of the lesson. When Min was summoned for a word, it was invariably to be told how brilliantly she was doing and to listen to new plans with which she could forge ahead: advanced reading books, inter-school competitions, extra-curricular classes and so on.

But one look at Mrs MacDuff's face told Min that she wasn't about to receive a big pat on the back. In fact, when she pulled up the chair offered, she got a real dressing down.

Admittedly the lesson hadn't gone well, but they'd had to prick their fingers and examine their blood cells under the microscope. Anything involving blood always made Min unwell. Still, even she'd been surprised when she had to run out of the room and puke into a bin. But then she saw puking as an improvement on fainting.

However, here was Mrs MacDuff, peering at her over a pair of dark-framed glasses and issuing words like 'no natural aptitude' and 'time to reconsider options'. The teacher then began talking about A-level biology as being 'virtually impossible'.

'I know you work very, very hard, Min,' she had gone on. 'That's not the issue. But I'm beginning to believe that your efforts with us are misguided. Maybe biology is a lost cause for you and you need to play to your other strengths.'

A lost cause? A *lost cause*?

Min was fiddling with her hair as another girl ploughed on through her pages of *Lettres*. She'd never before been told she wasn't good at something. It was a genuine shock. Anyway, she was going to be a doctor. There was no back-up plan. There was no other plan! Hadn't she been given her first play stethoscope at the age of three?

Her parents wanted a family of doctors – though the children were free to choose whichever speciality they wished to follow within medicine. That had been made clear. But the doctor bit wasn't optional: that was why she was here; that was why three times a year she got on a jumbo jet to Scotland while the rest of her family made do without holidays and fancy clothes and treats.

How was she going to tell her parents about this? It wasn't possible. She wasn't going to be able to do it. Giving up biology was not an option. She would just have to figure out a way of working round her squeamishness and studying harder. If she knew all the other things there were to know, what would it matter if she couldn't cope with a blood cell or two?

The other thing worrying Min was that her running times were bad too: down five whole seconds on her times from three weeks ago. Five seconds! She wasn't going to make it on Sports Day. Lauren Gaitling from Year Five was going to beat her. She would be eating the dust kicked up by Lauren's £150 pair of aerodynamic, extra-cushioned spikes. Well, not that the St Jude's state-of-the-art running track (installed after extensive fund-raising through the St Jude's old girl network) had any dust.

'Asimina! What are you doing?' Madame's sharp voice cut across Min's fraught train of thought. 'You do not even have your book open!'

What Min might have said in her defence no one would ever know, because at that moment Jenny stood up: Jenny, who'd been upset and tearful for weeks; Jenny, who had now sparked all sorts of increasingly lurid rumours because no one yet knew what it was all about.

Now, she scrunched up the note she'd intercepted and announced loudly: 'It's none of your business! It's nobody's business! But to stop any more ridiculous rumours like this' – she threw the note across the room – 'my dad's lost his job, so I'm leaving St Jude's and moving to Burnside Academy.'

Ignoring the collective intakes of breath, Jenny picked up her school bag, walked over to the classroom door and went out, giving it a heartfelt slam.

'*Mais alors!*' was Madame's outraged response.

'That'll be handy for the debating competition,' Penny Boswell-Hackett commented.

When Gina and Niffy looked at Amy for an explanation for this remark, Amy just shrugged her shoulders and hissed, 'I don't know!'

Madame looked confused. Finally, after several moments of deliberation, she must have decided that she should at least make an attempt to bring Jenny back, so she left the room, giving Penny ample opportunity to enlighten Amy.

'Haven't you been told, you no-hoper?' Penny asked her loudly from the opposite side of the room.

Amy made no reply; did not even give the slightest sign that she'd heard this.

'*This House believes that private schools are a waste of money and a social divide unnecessary in modern Britain*,' Penny announced. 'That's what we're debating, loser!'

Then Penny couldn't resist going on to play her trump card: 'I had a little walkabout with Jason on Saturday night, but I wasn't interested in what he had on offer. Apparently that's how he felt about you.'

Chapter Thirteen

Amy sat alone at a corner table in the Arts Café. Her blonde hair was pulled up into a high ponytail and a dangling gold earring brushed against a cheek perfectly shaded with Mac blusher. On the table beside her was a second drained cup of cappuccino; in her hands was a copy of *Vogue*, which was no longer as interesting as when she'd started reading it forty minutes ago.

It had taken Amy four hours to get ready for this evening and now it was beginning to look like she'd wasted her time. Her hands were shaking slightly and she knew she was too nervous to have a third coffee – she'd be wired!

On the other side of the café she could hear her friends laughing and joking with Dermot and she wished she was with them, rather than stuck at this table on her own, posing, posing and posing as she waited for Jason to walk through the door. But then, if he *did* walk through the door, she wanted him to sit with her, not just join in the group.

Despite Penny's horrible claims, Jason had emailed Amy the day after the ball. Although he'd sounded casual, hadn't he just been disguising the fact that he was really keen to see her again? Amy felt sure this was the case. She believed that she could understand the real Jason: the person behind the handsome, cool and swaggering façade.

Might be at the Arts Café later. Can you come round? Might be fun to see you and your friends. J.

That's what he'd written. *Can you come round?* He'd definitely wanted her to be here. It hadn't felt like such an exaggeration to tell the dorm she had a date with him.

'So how old are you anyway?' Niffy was asking Dermot, who had returned to their table even though there were no empty cups to clear away, because he was enjoying the few moments of banter he could snatch with them during his busy shift.

'If you've just done your Highers,' Niffy went on, 'you must be older than you look.'

'Or a precocious genius,' Dermot reminded her.

'How old are you?' he countered. 'And since you're not drinking Irish coffees tonight, you can be honest with me.'

'You first!' Gina insisted. 'How old are you?'

'I'm sixteen, but I'm going to be seventeen next month.' He knew, as soon as he'd said it, just how embarrassing that sounded.

'Ooooh,' Niffy teased. 'I'm fifteen, Gina's fifteen . . . Maybe Dermot wants to send us a birthday card.'

'No! You want us to send you a card next month!' Gina teased.

'Never mind, never mind.' Dermot was blushing. 'I'd better pick up your empties and be getting on.' He looked around the table for an empty mug, but there still wasn't one.

'Leave mine alone.' Gina slapped his hand gently. 'I'm still drinking!'

'Look! Violence! The girl is attacking me!' Dermot joked. 'I have witnesses.'

'Nah,' Niffy assured him. 'We're on her side.'

'Oh, the dorm girls stick together, no matter what, do they?' Dermot asked. 'By the way, does your dorm have a name?'

Niffy's eyes narrowed. 'Why do you want to know?'

'Well, they have names, don't they? Dorms? Pink

dorm? Dewdrop dorm? That kind of thing?' He was trying hard to keep a straight face.

'If we tell you, we'll have to kill you,' Gina replied.

Dermot leaned across the table: his arm was almost touching Gina's and suddenly she felt all the hairs stand on end, from her wrist right up to the nape of her neck.

'Go on,' he insisted. 'Your secret is safe with me.'

'We can't tell you,' Gina said.

'Why not?'

'Because you'll laugh.'

'I will not,' he insisted.

'Will too!'

'Bet you a fiver I won't.'

'We're in Daffodil dorm,' Gina said, spilling the beans, sure it was worth five pounds.

Dermot paused, seemed to struggle with his mouth for a moment, then, turning abruptly on his heels, said, 'OK, I have to go now – catch you later.'

'Look!' Niffy spluttered coffee. 'I don't believe it! Lover boy is here!'

All four turned their heads to see Jason coming into the café with Angus and Charlie in tow behind him.

'Aha, not quite the romantic-table-for-two scenario

our golden girl had planned then,' Niffy said, raising an eyebrow.

Amy's head hadn't turned. If she had spotted Jason coming in, then she wasn't letting on. She was busy posing with her *Vogue* as if her life depended on it.

Niffy gave a wave and the three boys headed over in her direction.

'Amy is over there,' Niffy told Jason as soon as he was within earshot. 'I think she wanted some quiet time with you.'

When this brought loud guffaws from Charlie and Angus, Jason pulled up a chair and said, 'Tell her to come and join us.'

Gina got up to oblige and also to make sure that Charlie didn't even consider sitting next to her.

As she explained Jason's request to a distressed Amy, she couldn't help saying, 'I know he's good-looking, but – I'm sorry, Amy – he just acts like a complete dickhead . . . some of the time,' she added quickly, as if that made it any better.

Amy just glared at her, then picked up her bag and headed over to the crowded table.

'Hi, Amy,' was all Jason could manage; he gave a little wave. A wave!

Amy chose a seat as far away from him as possible and tried not to let anyone see that she was blushing to the roots of her carefully styled hair and frantically squeezing back the tears forming in her eyes.

Her date was now a group event, the boys all going on about the party Charlie was hosting in his parents' house the following weekend (were they going to come, because he'd invited 'almost every other girl in their year' and, by the way, why hadn't they come to his house for tea the day after the ball?).

'Maybe you'd like to ask Min?' Gina snorted. 'If she was here she'd explain it to you.'

'Erm . . .' Charlie at least looked embarrassed.

'You'll have to work very hard to get us to forgive you for that,' Niffy said. 'For a start we want proper invitations. You know – something embossed with your coat of arms,' she teased, 'for the mantelpiece: *Charlie Fotheringham is at home.* No point having a party if you're not going to do it properly.'

'You think so?' Charlie seemed to be taking her seriously. 'That's a good idea. Invitations! I hadn't thought of that. Might be a good way of keeping out the crashers. Can't have the people's place getting trashed, you know. There are some good pieces in there.'

Pieces? Gina wondered what he could mean. Pieces of furniture? Works of art?

Dermot was obviously *delighted* to see three St Lennox boys move in on the dorm girls he was so interested in. He banged mugs down so hard and so rudely that coffee slopped onto the table.

'Clean that up!' Charlie barked at him.

Dermot reappeared with a wet dishcloth, which he lobbed at Charlie, saying, 'You wanted a cloth?'

'How dare you!' Charlie caught the wet cloth, sending a splatter of water into his face and over his clothes. 'That's it! Where's your boss? I'm going to get you fired.'

Dermot, suppressing a smile, turned and left the table as both Gina and Niffy tried to calm Charlie down.

'Look, I'm sure he didn't mean it,' Gina insisted. 'Please, don't make a big deal out of it.'

'For God's sake, let's drink up and get out of here,' Charlie said, wiping himself down with a couple of paper napkins. 'My brother's got a flat round the corner – we could go there,' he added. 'It's Saturday night: he's usually got something going on.'

'Good idea,' said Jason, uncrossing his long legs.

Which meant that Amy immediately said, 'Yeah, why not?'

Which meant that Niffy and Gina would have to tag along too.

Just twenty-five minutes in Charlie's big brother Hoagie's flat was enough to convince the girls that it was time to go.

No amount of Georgian splendour (cornicing, ancient floorboards, graceful windows) could make up for the obvious student squalor (days worth of unwashed dishes, grubby clothes on the floor, over-flowing ashtrays, and empty wine bottles in every corner). Gina had never seen anything like it. Her friends in LA all still lived with their parents, who tended to have maids. Her mouth hung open in astonishment and she refused to even sit down in case she caught something.

Hoagie, a great shambling bloke in a holey jumper, was watching a DVD with friends and didn't seem very pleased to see Charlie with two boys and three girls in tow.

Angus made an effort to jolly everyone along: 'Hoagie, love what you've done with the place! It's sort of wrecked Budapest nightclub meets nineteen nineties grunge.'

An attempt at tea was made, but as no one could find any clean mugs or any milk – or, in fact, any tea bags – it had to be abandoned.

'If you want booze, you'll have to go and get your own,' Hoagie shouted at them from the sitting room.

'You know what? I think we should leave. Amy?' Gina's sharp tone of voice made it clear that they were going, even if Amy had managed to wheedle herself a chair next to Jason's.

Not that Jason had noticed. He was too busy going through Hoagie's CD collection. He'd offered to put on some music but fifteen minutes later he still couldn't decide which album would least offend his complicated sense of cool.

In the taxi home, Amy couldn't stop reliving every moment of the evening, casting Jason in as flattering a light as possible. 'He wants to see me next weekend,' she told her friends. 'Asked if we were going to Charlie's . . .'

The other girls were not convinced

'But did he snog you goodbye?' Niffy wanted to know. 'Because if he did, I would take that as a sign that he's definitely interested.'

'Well . . . erm . . . we kissed on the cheeks, but that's because he's actually quite shy. I think that's why he brought his friends along and didn't want to sit with me at the other table.'

Gina and Niffy exchanged doubtful glances. Then Niffy announced out of the blue that she thought Angus was 'completely hilarious', which earned her a round of whistles and cheers.

'I don't fancy him!' she insisted loudly, but there was much teasing and in-depth discussion about the suitability of Angus as a boyfriend, and when Gina and Niffy walked into the boarding-house sitting room to sign in, Mrs Knebworth's first question took them completely by surprise.

'How was the film?' she asked, causing the two girls to look at each other in panic.

'Oh . . . we really enjoyed it, didn't we?' Niffy answered first, managing to sound casual, but looking desperately at Gina in the hope that she could remember something about the film they'd agreed to pretend to go and see.

'It wasn't bad. Quite cheesy,' Gina ventured, but suspected she'd sounded too nervous. Why hadn't Min gone with them tonight? She was the one who could be relied upon to prime them all with reviews and plot details.

'Anyway' – Niffy attempted a hurried getaway – 'we should be—'

But the Neb cut across her with a clear and unmistakable: 'So what did you go and see?' She took her eyes off the television screen so the girls had her full unwanted attention.

Suddenly Gina remembered the title of one of the films Min had recommended ... *China* ... *China Something* ...

'*China Doll*,' she blurted out, almost certain that this was the name of the film.

'Oh yes, with ... umm ... what's her name?' Mrs Knebworth's head bent slightly to one side, as if this was the most interesting conversation she'd had all day.

Suddenly Gina was suspicious. Was this just chitchat, or was the Neb trying to test them?

She realized she was going to have to answer because Niffy's face looked completely blank.

'Oh ... I can never remember her name ...' Gina began. 'Reese Witherspoon?' She couldn't help crossing her fingers behind her back because she had no idea who the heroine was or if *China Doll* was even actually a movie. 'It was fun,' she added, with something that was supposed to look like a casual shrug.

'I'm absolutely bushed!' Niffy exclaimed with an exaggerated yawn, trying to get them out of there as quickly as possible.

'And where's Amy?' the Neb asked next.

'She's just gone to the pantry to put the kettle on – shall we sign her in too? Or do you want her to come in?'

'Oh, just sign her in and head up to bed.' The Neb turned her eyes back to the screen. 'I believe you.' A little smile flashed across her face.

As soon as Mrs Knebworth heard Gina and Niffy's footsteps receding along the corridor, she pushed herself up out of her chair and headed in the direction of the pantry.

This was a little place off the dining room stocked with tea bags, instant coffee, hot chocolate powder, water and fruit, where the girls were allowed to go and make themselves a drink or grab a snack in between official meal times.

'Oh, hello, Mrs Knebworth,' Amy greeted her. 'The kettle's just boiled – do you want me to make you a tea?'

'Yes, that would be kind,' said the Neb. 'So, another

trip to the cinema?' she went on. 'And what did you and the girls go to tonight?'

'Oh . . .' Amy hesitated. She'd been so wrapped up in preparing for a close encounter of the Jason kind that she had barely listened to Min's read-through of the film reviews. 'Oh, erm . . . didn't they say? You know what my memory's like.' She tried to sound jokey and tapped at the side of her head.

'No.' Mrs Knebworth's little eyes were peering out at Amy from her pale and pudgy face.

'Erm . . . it was . . .' Amy racked her brain for any mention of any film that she'd heard recently . . . Hello . . . just any film at all. Absolutely nothing came to mind. She could feel her face start to flush.

'*Party Girl*,' she decided on finally, pretty sure that this wasn't a film – it was something she'd made up. But Amy hated blushing and she hated being interrogated, so she'd decided to get out of there as quickly as possible. 'Pretty good,' she added. 'Gina loved it.' Then she picked up her mug and headed out of the room, completely forgetting about the cup she'd offered to make for the Neb.

Mrs Knebworth found a tea bag and poured boiling water into the mug Amy had set out for her. After swirling it about with a teaspoon, she fished the bag out and carried it over to the bin; next she poured in a drop of milk and stirred slowly.

Now she would take a few sips . . . take a moment. Then she would head over to Daffodil dorm and listen to some more feeble excuses and fibs about what had gone on tonight.

By the time she opened the dorm door, Amy had an explanation at the ready: 'It was *China Doll* . . . they just keep referring to her as the "party girl", so I got confused . . .'

'And I don't know how I muddled Reese Witherspoon up with Scarlett Johansson,' said Gina, but she didn't sound nearly as convincing as Amy.

Mrs Knebworth's eyes narrowed dangerously. 'Are you girls under the impression that I am stupid?' she asked slowly and icily, clearly in no mood to have the wool pulled over her eyes.

'No!' Amy was the first to answer. 'Of course not.'

'Well then, don't bother telling me any more fibs about the cinema.' Then, in a low and commanding tone, she asked, 'Just where exactly have the three of you been tonight?'

It was Gina who broke the silence. 'Look, I'm sorry, we didn't go to the cinema – but all we did was go to the Arts Café for coffee. I mean, it's hardly breaking the law, is it? Why do we always have to say we're going to the cinema?'

The sharp intakes of breath from Amy, Niffy and Mrs Knebworth let Gina know immediately that she had said the wrong thing.

'*Always?*' Mrs Knebworth repeated. 'So you *always* say you're going to the cinema, do you? When, in fact, you're going out and hanging around in places like the Arts Café where they sell . . . *alcohol*!' There was no mistaking the outrage heaped onto this last word.

'We had coffee!' Gina insisted, but Niffy and Amy already knew it was too late.

'You are gated!' came the Neb's verdict.

'For how long?' There was a pleading tone to Amy's question.

'Until further notice! Now get to bed, all of you!' With that Mrs Knebworth turned and left the dorm, slamming the door behind her.

'Charlie's party!' Amy wailed.

'She wouldn't have let us go anyway,' said Niffy.

'We'd have thought of something!' Amy insisted.

'Not any more,' Gina said.

As the light was clicked off in Daffodil dorm, Gina looked up at the ceiling and thought not of her mother, her brother and her home, five thousand miles away. She thought of Mrs Knebworth and infuriating school rules, and itched with injustice at the punishment that had just been issued. Yes, as every day passed, Gina was becoming more and more of a Daffodil.

Chapter Fourteen

Miss Ballantyne was handing back essays. She was moving slowly round the classroom, dishing out comments along with the marked pages.

'Quite nice, Willow, but a little short. I'd liked to have seen more.'

'Suzie, your spelling is atrocious – if you can spell that.'

'Penny . . . a lovely piece of work.'

As Gina's essay flopped down onto her desk, she could already make out the bright red circled C on the top page. The only subject at St Jude's in which Gina seemed to be making any progress was English.

'Some effort is going to have to be made, Gina Peterson, or you will be seeing a list of exam results just like your mother's,' came the stern rebuke.

'Like my *mother's*?' The disbelief in Gina's voice was obvious.

'Indeed.'

Miss Ballantyne was already moving on, next essay in hand, next comment at the ready.

'My mother was a straight-A student,' Gina said defiantly. 'You must be confused.'

She heard one of those disdainful 'humph' sounds that the St Jude's staff seemed to specialize in. Miss Ballantyne raised her eyebrows, sniffed, then slowly, and for maximum effect, said witheringly, 'I suppose that's what she told you, is it?'

This produced a flurry of giggles around the class, and Gina, blushing furiously, decided to back off. What was going on? There were many things in her life she couldn't be sure of, but the fact that her mother was brilliant and had done amazingly at school and university was *not* one of them. That was a definite. Miss Ballantyne was wrong. Miss Ballantyne was a bitter old cow. Miss Ballantyne . . .

Amy nudged her. 'Don't believe a word she says,' she whispered. 'She's mental. A founder member of Morningside Ladies Say No To Homosexuals, apparently. They outed two vicars.'

The idea of the respectable ladies of Edinburgh's Morningside ganging together against vicars with

Miss Ballantyne at the fore was just enough to make Gina's eyes stop swimming.

All at once the feeling she'd had for a little while now – the feeling that maybe she could fit in and get along here – was gone. Now, all she could think about was how much she missed home – and her family too. When the history lesson was over, there would be no going home to hide in her room, stretch out across her bed or turn the music on loud. She wouldn't be running a luxuriously deep bath, or trying on different outfits, calling her best friends or going over to one of their houses. No. When school ended today, she would hoist her school bag onto her back and trudge over to the boarding house, where she would be surrounded for the rest of the day with the chatter and babble of other girls she still didn't know really well. If she wanted any peace and quiet in the boarding house, she would have to retreat to the large study room and do her homework.

'Oh dear,' Mrs Knebworth sighed as Amy, Gina, Niffy and Min came into the front hall. 'Couldn't help noticing that you've been invited to a party – such a shame you won't be able to go.' There wasn't the slightest sympathy in her voice though.

'The cow has been reading our mail!' Amy shouted in fury as soon as the Neb was out of earshot. She went over to the hall table where all the letters to the boarders were laid out, and spotted the postcard addressed to 'Amy, Niffy and the Yank'. Turning it over, she read the elaborate copperplate writing out loud: '*Charlie Fotheringham is at home from eight p.m. Please come – it'll be cool.*'

'*The Yank?*' Gina exclaimed. 'God, he's such a jerk!'

'Penny's already told me she's going – along with just about everyone else in the entire year,' Amy added. She didn't repeat the really annoying thing Penny had said to her: 'Oh, you won't be there? Shame . . . Maybe Jason will turn his attention to someone else then. Isn't he quite the ladies' man?'

Min saw the thin blue airmail envelope addressed to her lying on the table and snatched it up. Without saying anything, she rushed off to the dorm to read the contents in private.

As soon as Niffy opened the dorm door, she could see that all was not well with Min. Her friend was lying across her bed with the airmail letter scrunched up in her hand and tears running down her face.

'Min! What is it?' Niffy demanded, rushing over, Gina and Amy hot on her heels.

Min wiped a hand across her face and just handed Niffy the page. Struggling with the cramped, squiggly handwriting, Niffy began to read aloud:

'*Dearest Asimina, Your father and I were . . . shacked?*'

'*Shocked*,' Min corrected.

'*Shocked to get your last letter. Not do biology A-level? There is no question of this, Asimina. No question. Why are you not working harder at your studies? We have always planned for you to follow our family's proud medical tradition . . .*' Niffy looked up from the page. 'Oh dear,' she said. 'I think we know where this is going.'

Min burst into a fresh bout of tears.

'Don't worry,' Amy insisted, sitting down beside Min and patting her on the shoulder. 'We'll think of something. Honestly. My dad always says there's no problem that can't be solved. You've just got to step back and look at the bigger picture.'

'I need to be a doctor!' Min wailed. 'I need a really good biology A-level to be a doctor and I know I'm not going to get that.'

'Do you want to be a doctor, Min?' Gina asked.

'Of course!' Min hissed.

'But the sight of blood makes you either puke or faint,' Niffy reminded her.

'That's just . . . that's just . . . a minor detail!' Min spluttered, but then dissolved into another flood of tears.

Chapter Fifteen

Although it was close to 10 p.m., late June in Edinburgh meant there was no sign of the daylight fading yet, so Amy and Niffy sat out on the fire escape, still moaning about having to spend Saturday night in the boarding house while everyone else they knew was at Charlie's house party. They were each holding a tooth mug containing the remains of a half-bottle of M&S dessert wine, bought from Sideshow Mel at an inflated price.

'This is just so mince!' Amy complained. 'Jason is going!'

'How do you know?' Niffy asked. 'Do you think this wine is meant to taste slightly minty? Or did I not rinse the mugs out enough?'

'He emailed,' Amy said, turning to Niffy with a secretive little smile.

'He sent you another email? Good grief! It must be

love,' Niffy exclaimed. 'What did he say this time? *Hi,
Whatsyourname, could you be at Charlie's party in case
I decide to drop by and need someone to ignore?*'

'Shut up, Nif! Why do you always have to put him
down like this?'

'Dunno, Amy! Why do you always have to build
him up to god-like status? He's just another dorky
sixteen-year-old who just happens to have won the
lottery in the looks department. Doesn't make him any
better than the rest of them.'

'Oh, listen to you, Miss Mature.'

'Neb alert.' Niffy pointed down to the housemistress's bedroom window, where a curtain was
being drawn.

'Thought you said she couldn't see us?'

'Don't think she can,' Niffy replied. 'But it's much
lighter now.'

'Well, she can't tonight, believe me.' Amy's secretive
smile crossed her face again. 'I've taken all her
spectacles.'

'All of them?' Niffy stared at her incredulously. '*All?*'

'Oh yes, every single one of her four pairs,' Amy
said triumphantly.

'Even the pair she was wearing? When and how did
you do that?'

'Well' – Amy leaned back, enjoying the confession – 'I rounded up the three spares in the course of the afternoon.'

'You went into her rooms?' Even Niffy sounded shocked.

'Uh-huh – then, tonight, when she had her little evening snooze in front of the telly, I got hold of the last pair.'

'And where are they all now?'

'In the one place she won't look.'

'Which is?'

'Min's chest of drawers.'

'Does Min know this?'

'Actually, she does. She said I could use it for one night only but I had to give them back tomorrow. That was my plan anyway: sneak them all back into strange places. Make the Neb think she's losing her marbles.'

'Shhh, I can hear music,' Niffy said.

'Maybe it's coming all the way from Charlie's house,' Amy sighed. 'Maybe Jason finally found a CD to put on.'

'Yeah, right.' Niffy's sarcasm was obvious. 'No, I think there's a concert on at Murrayfield. Listen . . .'

'A house party! A concert! It's all happening out there! And where are we? We're stuck up a fire escape!

It's so unfair,' Amy wailed. 'We're prisoners. In our teenage prime!'

It was after midnight and much darker outside when Niffy stirred in her sleep. She'd dreamed of a tapping sound: *Tap tap tappity-tap*.

There it was again.

Tap. Tap. Tap.

Niffy sat up in bed. It was coming from the window leading to the fire escape. She tried to consider a possible explanation. Branch tapping against the glass? No, too high up. Window rattling in its frame? Don't think so.

The tapping began again, and this time it was accompanied by several giggles.

'Amy!' Niffy hissed and reached over to give her friend a shake. 'Amy! There's someone at the window!'

It only took a moment for Amy to go from deeply asleep to wide awake. 'At the window?' she repeated in a whisper.

They strained their ears, and several seconds later the tapping started up again. Along with a strange clinking noise.

'That sounds like chains!' Amy whispered in

horror. 'We're about to be tortured! We have to phone the police. *Now!*'

'Shhh!' Niffy insisted. 'It sounds like bottles. I heard a giggle as well. Do serial killers giggle?'

'Yes!' Amy's eyes were wide with fright.

'Amy!' a lowered voice called out from the other side of the window. 'Are you there?'

Amy leaped out of bed and grabbed Niffy's arm in fear. 'Help! Someone out there's come to get me!' she shrieked, waking up Gina and Min in the process.

Niffy began to giggle. 'Silly old tart,' she said and got out of bed. Striding towards the window, she put her hand on the blind to open it.

'Noooooo!' Amy warned.

But Niffy had revealed two dark figures hunched on the fire escape, clinking, giggling and tapping.

Amy was still crouched down behind her bed, but Niffy calmly took hold of the brass handles and flung the window wide open. As soon as she saw who was out there, she began to laugh.

'Oh, it's you! How romantic! Would you like to come in?'

'How kind,' came the reply.

As soon as Amy heard those words, she frantically ran her hands through her hair, deeply regretting her choice of ratty old pyjamas for bed tonight.

'Jason?' she asked the figure as it stepped down from the window ledge and into the darkened room. 'What the hell are you doing here?'

A second boy was clambering down behind Jason, carrying the bulging plastic bag responsible for the clinking sounds.

'Angus and I thought we'd just drop by,' Jason informed the room casually, 'since you couldn't make the party. A little bird told us you live at the top of the fire escape.'

Gina switched on a bedside light to take a better look at the intruders and convince herself that no, she wasn't dreaming. Min sat up but shyly pulled the covers right up to her chin.

There was something of an awkward pause as everyone adjusted to the shock of the situation. The girls were caught somewhere between pleasant surprise at the visit and fear that they would get caught and instantly expelled. Well, make that: Niffy was delighted by this new adventure, Amy was stunned that Jason had just walked in through her window, and Min and Gina were terrified.

'How about a beer?' Angus asked cheerfully. 'We brought along a few bottles and even a bottle opener.'

He took this out of his coat pocket with a flourish, then sat down on the corner of Min's bed and began to rummage around in his bag.

'Good idea.' Jason chose to sit on Amy's bed and immediately put an arm around her. 'Hello there,' he purred. 'Pleased to see me?'

With a jolt of astonished happiness, Amy leaned in to kiss him on the cheek. He smelled beery and she wondered if he was already a bit drunk.

'Right . . . well, I think we'll leave the love birds to it in the corner while we crack on over here,' Angus decided as he popped the tops off four bottles and handed them out.

Although Min and Gina shook their heads, Angus wouldn't hear of it. 'We've come all this way!' he insisted. 'The least you can do is have a drink with me!'

As soon as Niffy's first bottle was almost empty, she gave a great burp of appreciation: Min looked shocked while Angus laughed heartily.

'Can we be heard up here?' he wanted to know. 'Should we be partying quietly?'

'We should keep it down, just to be on the safe side,' Niffy told him. 'We don't want everyone else on this floor joining in.'

'Yes we do!' Angus replied. 'We've got plenty of bottles!'

'How is Charlie's party going?' Gina asked.

'It is utterly fantastic! The place is packed; he's got a DJ in, tons of booze. Tons! Mind you, he's had to hide the key to the basement because his old man's got bottles of really good stuff stashed away down there.'

'So why did you come all the way out here to see us,' Niffy wondered, 'if there's such a great party going on in town? Especially you, Mr Party Animal, Mr G-Pants.' She gave a throaty giggle. 'Have you been thwinging your thong?'

Angus gave her a cheeky smile. 'That's my party piece. Did you hear about it? We came because we were missing you, of course,' he added.

'Hmmm.' Niffy sounded unconvinced. 'The real reason?' she pressed.

'That *is* the real reason: we love St Jude's boarders – they're the best,' Angus insisted. 'Sexiest schoolgirls in Edinburgh.'

'So absolutely nothing whatsoever to do with something like . . . let's see . . . a bet?' Niffy asked, moving closer to Angus and nudging him in the ribs as encouragement.

'I quite like that,' he told her, meaning the nudging.

'Confess!' she instructed.

'Well . . .' Angus looked a little uncomfortable and began to rummage through his shaggy hair.

'Aha. What's the deal? No, don't tell me – you have to photograph us in our pyjamas with your mobile phone maybe? Take the picture back to the party as a trophy? And what do you get?' Niffy urged.

'Well . . . it's a bit more complicated than that,' Angus admitted.

'Go on,' Gina insisted.

Angus glanced over his shoulder at Jason, to make sure he wasn't being overheard, but Jason was a little too preoccupied with snogging Amy to be paying much attention to the rest of them.

'Well,' he began in a whisper, 'if we can persuade two of you to come back to the party with us, everyone in the room has to give us ten pounds.'

Niffy cackled. 'I like it,' she said. 'And you'd split the money with us?'

Angus had the decency to blush.

'You weren't going to tell us!' Niffy was outraged and smacked Angus on the arm. 'You scumbags!'

She glanced over at her friend, whose jaw was just about wrapped round Jason's.

'So that's why Jasey's busy working on Amy, is it?'

Angus nodded and took another swig of beer.

'Do you know what I would really like?' Jason's warm beer breath was tickling Amy's neck, making the hairs at the nape and all the way down her arm stand on end.

'What?' she whispered back.

He put his lips right up against her ear so she could just make out the words: 'I'd like you to show me your teddies.'

Her teddies?

It was kind of sweet. But did he really think she still cuddled up with a toy at night? Well, there was one small, special little bear she still kept, but not in her bed. Jimjim was in her top drawer, safely tucked in under her smalls. And even Jason wasn't going to get a look at him.

She turned and whispered in Jason's ear, 'But I haven't got any.'

He pulled back from her and, no longer whispering, asked in surprise, 'What do you mean?'

'I haven't got any teddies,' she said.

'Not *teddies*!' Jason spluttered. 'Titties! I want to see your titties.'

'Oh!'

And then she heard it.

There was absolutely no mistaking the slow screech of the fire door being pulled open on its rusty old hinge.

'Twenty-second warning!' she shrieked at the room. 'The *Neb*!'

'*The Neb!*' Gina repeated in horror.

Immediately, Min cut the bedside light and they fled round the room in darkness, kicking the bag of bottles under a bed, pulling Angus and Jason towards the window.

'Nine . . . eight . . .' Amy was counting in a terrified whisper. 'There isn't time!'

Angus, sensibly, dived under Min's bed. Jason, to Gina's astonishment, dived straight *into* hers.

'Covers up!' he ordered.

There was no time to argue.

She lay down with the duvet pulled up over them both, her heart drumming in her chest, because how would she ever be able to explain away being caught with a boy actually *in her bed*! Her cheeks were already burning with the shame and humiliation of it. The horrible rumours would follow her all the way home to California.

Clearly Jason wasn't worried, because as they lay in

the darkness listening to the heavy footsteps in the corridor, waiting out the final seconds before Mrs Knebworth pulled open the dorm door to find them, his fingers found the gap between her pyjama bottoms and vest top. Then his warm hand began to ease across her stomach, his fingers boldly moving upwards. Gina wanted to elbow him or kick him hard but she was too terrified to move a muscle.

His forefinger was, with the most delicate of touches, stroking her nipple, which immediately, disobediently, sprang to a point. Eyes scrunched up in the darkness, Gina had to register the other reason why she didn't move, didn't even breathe: because this felt as magical as imaginary fireworks going off against her skin.

But this was Jason! Right thing, wrong person . . . very right . . . very. Very wrong.

The door opened and there was no mistaking the voice which broke into the room. Gina didn't even dare to breathe, let alone try to move Jason's hand away.

'What is going on?' the Neb demanded in her most severe tone. 'Just what is going on?' she repeated.

No one said anything, although Gina thought she could hear Min moan quietly with fright.

'I have looked everywhere,' Mrs Knebworth barked into the silence. 'I have looked in every single place I can think of and every single one of my four pairs of glasses is missing. All four! It just can't be a co-incidence! I no longer care if it's the middle of the night. I know this must have something to do with the fact that three people in this room have been gated for the weekend! Amy!' she shouted. 'Do something! Get me my glasses! I don't care if you're asleep or not.'

There was still silence. No one wanted to make the slightest move in case the Neb reached for the light switch and everything was discovered.

The silence went on, with Mrs Knebworth just standing there right in the doorway in a floor-length quilted dressing gown. Her hair was up on end and, silhouetted against the light from the corridor, she looked like some huge crazed opera diva.

'Mrs Knebworth,' came Min's trembling voice finally, 'I can get your glasses for you. D'you want to just give me a few minutes, and I'll be right down with them.'

There was a long pause during which Angus hugged the burning burp tight within his windpipe, Jason silently took a gentle squeeze of Gina's breast and Amy prayed that she would not have to explain a word of this to her dad, who would never forgive her for getting kicked out of school over boys.

'Very well then,' Mrs Knebworth said finally. 'I'll wait for you downstairs, Asimina. But quick as you can. And I will deal with the rest of you in the morning.'

The door shut, but it wasn't until they heard her footsteps in the corridor and the screech of the fire door closing that anyone dared to make a move.

Min opened one of her drawers in the dark and extracted the spectacles Amy had hidden there. Angus rolled out from under the bed and, to Amy's horror, Jason reappeared from beneath Gina's covers.

Gina heard Amy's gasp and immediately looked round at her and offered her a shrug of the shoulders. This wasn't exactly her fault!

'Go!' Niffy instructed in a whisper, hauling open the window. 'Go very quickly, while she's still waiting for Min at the bottom of the stairs.'

'What about the bet?' Angus, one leg over the windowsill, wanted to know. 'We could make five hundred quid – maybe more.'

Chapter Sixteen

'I think we may have made a mistake coming here,' Niffy admitted to Gina as they both sat under a table, hidden behind folds of tablecloth.

'What?' Gina moved in closer so that she could hear her friend above the pounding music threatening to shake the precious ornaments from the shelves in this ornate Georgian dining room.

'This was a mistake!' Niffy shouted back.

'Oh! Now you tell me! What have I been saying for like the last hour and a half!' Gina replied heatedly. 'This was *your* idea.'

And that was true. Niffy had said she wanted to sneak out to Charlie's party for the money. Gina partly believed her, because Niffy never seemed to have any money, but she also suspected their risky night out had something to do with the fact that lately there was a little sparkle in Niffy's eyes whenever Angus was around.

Amy had flatly refused to come. The three of them had argued in angry whispers.

'You think I'd go with her,' Amy had stormed, pointing at Gina, 'after what she's done!'

'What have I done?' Gina had demanded, horrified.

'Oh, I'm sorry,' Amy had snapped back. 'Jason was *in your bed*! Didn't you notice?'

This had totally riled Gina. 'You think I wanted him there? He jumped in beside me! And you know what? The creep felt me up! That's what he's really like, for your information! A creep! Isn't it about time you figured that out?'

But Gina was embarrassed to find herself blushing because, creep or not, her skin still crackled and tingled at the thought of him.

'It wasn't Gina's fault!' Niffy had waded into the argument.

This only made Amy even more furious. 'Don't you say anything! Don't make it worse! How dare you be on her side!' Then she'd flung herself dramatically onto her bed, pulled her duvet over her head and begun to sob.

Partly to get away from the dorm and Amy's sobbing, and partly because she was so grateful for Niffy's support, Gina had recklessly decided to join her on the night-time escape from the boarding house.

They'd both pulled on jeans, boots and tops, then snuck as quietly as possible down the fire escape.

It was close to one o'clock in the morning, and they'd jogged for twenty minutes through sleepy streets until they reached the imposing row of town-houses. It wasn't hard to pick out number 15 – blazing with light and noise – where Charlie was 'at home' for friends.

The girls hadn't even had to ring the bell; they'd just walked in through the open double door, past the soaring spiral staircase, and wandered through the three enormous ground-floor rooms of Charlie's family home.

Gina had never been in a house like this. Well, not a genuine one – some mock Californian versions maybe – but this place! Even with teenagers lounging on sofas, leaning against walls and sprawled across the floor, the house was breathtaking. Cornicing decorated the high ceilings like icing, brooding oil paintings of stags and ancestors loomed down from the dark walls, and everywhere Gina looked there was ornate antique stuff: Chinese vases, carved mahogany chairs, faded chintz upholstery, leather-bound books,

and wide floorboards which bore the scuffs of generations of feet.

Charlie must have been out of his mind to think he
could get away with holding a party here. Look at the
rug over there! It was some ancient Persian work of
art. How was he going to get cigarette burns and wine
stains out of that?

They'd only seen Charlie for a moment. He'd
rushed past them, not even noticing them, shouting
out to no one in particular, 'I did say no smoking in
the drawing room. Come on now, there's a garden
at the back, for heaven's sake!'

But then they'd spotted Penny and friends and
decided that a spell under the dining-room table
would be more sensible than running the risk of
bumping into them.

'I don't trust her,' Niffy explained once they were
safely under the genuine Jacobean oak table. 'She
could photograph us with her phone and somehow
make sure it got back to the Neb.'

After several minutes had passed, they began to
realize how much fun it was to be the invisible guests
at a party.

'There's Llewellyn admiring the Fotheringham
family portraits,' Niffy noticed.

They watched as Penny's boyfriend finished his tour of the art in the room, then headed over to the buffet table to heap a generous serving onto his plate. He picked up a fork, but paused and brought it up to his face to take a closer look. After he'd scrutinized it closely, he slipped it into his trouser pocket, then picked up several other pieces of cutlery and slipped those in too.

'He's stealing the silverware?' Gina whispered to Niffy.

'Hey! You! What the hell do you think you're doing?' Charlie bounded up to him.

'What do you mean?' Llewellyn fired back in a voice no less posh, despite his comprehensive school education.

'I saw you put our cutlery in your pocket. You're stealing it, aren't you? Even some grubby Burnside Academy boy like you can spot crested silver cutlery, can't you?'

Charlie, possibly exhausted by the stress of fag burns on the Aubusson, red wine on the staircase sisal and the four teenage girls who had trampolined straight through the heirloom four-poster upstairs, pushed Llewellyn hard on the shoulder so that he wobbled and nearly overbalanced.

Gina nudged Niffy. 'This is going to be good,'

'Look, you prat,' Llewellyn shot at Charlie, 'I put your precious cutlery in my pocket so I could carry some for me and some for my girlfriend into the other room, OK?' With that, he pulled the silverware out of his pocket.

Both Niffy and Gina strained to see what was in his hands. It did indeed look like a perfectly credible two knives and two forks.

'Get over yourself,' Llewellyn added, jabbing a finger into Charlie's chest. 'It's just stuff.' He waved his hand around the room. 'It's all just stuff. It doesn't make you any better or any worse than the rest of us. Property is theft, anyway.'

Niffy rolled her eyes at Gina. 'Blimey, I didn't realize he was a communist as well as a comprehensive boy.'

Llewellyn began to walk out of the room. Charlie just let him, without adding any further insult.

It was then that Gina and Niffy first noticed the couple in the big armchair in the corner. They were wrapped round each other, his hands up her top, her hands down the front of his trousers.

'Euwww . . .' Gina was taken aback. 'Don't they have a home to go to?'

Just then the faces broke apart to catch their breath,

long enough for the girls hidden under the table to see who they were.

'Now that's depressing,' was Niffy's verdict.

Gina nodded. 'He's a total creep. What did I say? And how come she's out so late?'

'Maybe she's staying with a day girl for the weekend,' Niffy replied.

They watched as Jason and Sideshow Mel went back to their frantic snogathon.

'Remind me not to invite Amy to Mel's room for that talk,' Niffy said.

'Oh, look at them,' Gina whispered. 'I'm worried they're going to have sex right in front of us. We do not want to see that.'

Niffy peered out. 'I don't suppose there's much point reminding him about the bet now, is there? I haven't even been able to find Angus.' She sounded a little down about this, which could have meant she was sorry not to see Angus . . . or, more likely, that she was sorry not to see the money.

'Might have been hard to get people to pay up though,' she concluded and took another peek at Jason and Mel from under the tablecloth. 'We should pay more attention – we might learn something.'

When Gina seemed to go pale at the thought of

this, Niffy couldn't help asking, 'You don't really seem to be as much into boys as I was expecting you to be.'

'What? Because I'm American?' Gina sounded offended.

'Well . . . you go to a mixed school and all that . . . It must be a bit easier, getting to know boys.'

Gina leaned back, sipping from the small plastic cup of wine she'd managed to bring to the under-the-table party. 'I'm worried Squid Boy has put me off kissing for life,' she confided. 'I can't tell you how horrible it was . . . like he'd put a warm frog in my mouth.'

'Oh no!' Niffy cringed. 'Yuck! You're putting me off my drink!'

'I don't know if I ever want to go there again . . . which probably makes me a little strange,' Gina went on. 'How am I going to go out with anyone if I don't want to kiss them?'

'You know, I don't think you should worry about it,' Niffy reassured her. 'I'm sure if you're kissing someone you're totally mad about, their tongue won't feel so warm . . . or froggy! It will probably feel' – here her voice went into advert voiceover mode – '*like an amazingly intimate adventure.*'

Gina began to giggle. 'Speaking from experience, are you?'

'Oh yeah. Absolutely. But aren't Californian boys much, much better than British ones?' Niffy asked. 'Aren't they all fit and tanned, with a lot less hang-ups.'

'We have all kinds over there too, you know. It's not really like they made out in *Buffy*.' Gina took another sip of wine.

'Do you miss home a lot?' Niffy wondered.

For a few moments Gina thought about home. She thought about her mother, heading off to work, car roof down, sunglasses on, hair flying in the breeze. She thought about Menzie and Mick listening to music turned up loud in the SUV as they set off in the other direction to Menzie's school. Gina thought about her school and about Paula, Maddison and Ria. They emailed often, but she didn't know where they were partying this weekend . . . and who else would be there? She imagined the smell of orange trees and salty beach air, suntan lotion and wet swimsuits. The taste of grape-flavoured Slush Puppies . . . or blueberry pancakes, warm, with a scoop of ice cream sliding off the top, the berries hot and mushy inside.

Finally, feeling her eyes swim with tears, she managed to say, 'Yeah . . . I really, really miss home. Can't wait to go back.'

'Well, that's good,' was Niffy's verdict. Then came a

more unexpected question: 'When did your parents divorce?'

'Oh!' Gina was startled by this. Her parents had split up so long ago, nobody at home ever referred to it. 'They didn't get divorced,' she explained to Niffy. 'They never married. They were together for a few years, had me, my dad left, and that was kind of it. He doesn't exactly keep in touch. Mick's great though,' she added. 'I call him Mick but he is kind of my dad.'

'I think my parents should get divorced,' Niffy said in response to this, 'but they won't because they'd have to sell up and the Hall's—'

'Been in your family for five generations.' Gina finished Niffy's sentence with a smile. 'Why don't they open it to the public?' she suggested. 'Make some money that way?'

'Oh God.' Niffy let out a sigh. 'They do! Mum shows people round our kitchen and bedrooms and stuff and it is just so totally embarrassing.'

Gina giggled. Somehow, that wasn't quite how she'd pictured it.

And then their chat was interrupted by the sound of Jason exclaiming with some confusion, 'Sorry! You know what? I have to go!'

Niffy lifted the tablecloth so they could look out again.

They saw Jason scrambling up from the chair and tugging his top down and his trousers up.

'I don't know what I was thinking,' he told Mel before hurrying out of the room.

Neither he nor the two girls under the table were prepared for the volume on Mel's outraged screech of 'Whaaaaat!!'

Chapter Seventeen

Amy and Niffy had pulled chairs across to the dorm window so they could watch Min running out on the track. No mention had been made of their row the night before. Amy had just shaken Niffy awake with the words: 'Good party? Did you see Jason and Angus? Make loads of money?'

Once Niffy had informed her, 'No, no and definitely no' (she wasn't going to be the one to mention anything about Jason), Amy hadn't mentioned the party again, or the Gina and Jason incident.

Even making allowances for the fact that it was Sunday afternoon and she'd had an interrupted sleep the night before, Min seemed to be running very slowly.

'She's all hunched,' said Amy. 'She looks like she's got the troubles of the world on her shoulders.'

'She's definitely got troubles,' Niffy agreed.

'I think she's depressed. Depressed people get like this. All slow and anxious and obsessive.'

'You read that, did you, Amy?' Niffy teased. 'In a magazine or something?'

'Shut up!' Amy replied. 'We need to help Min.'

She was already trying to help Min. Whenever she'd had a chance to get onto the boarding-house computer, she'd been searching the Internet – Googling the words 'medicine and physics' and looking carefully through the array of results. Somewhere in there, she was sure, she was going to find an answer for Min.

Her eye fell on the plastic bag bundled up under Min's bed. 'Oh my God, Niffy!' she exclaimed. 'We have to get rid of the beer bottles!'

'Bloody hell!'

The two girls left Min dragging herself round the running track. They pulled the bag out: inside there were four empties and at least eight full bottles.

'Where are we going to put these?' Amy asked anxiously.

They both knew that Mrs Knebworth looked carefully through the dorms during school hours, searching for contraband and secrets.

'Where's the Neb right now?' Niffy asked.

Amy looked at her watch. 'Three-thirty. Hard to say. Maybe in her rooms or maybe prowling about downstairs.'

'We need to get this down to the sitting room without her seeing us. You go on ahead as lookout and I'll follow behind with the bottles.'

'The sitting room?' Amy asked.

'Yeah – we stash them in the piano down there, then on Monday I leave a note for Agnes asking her to sneak them out of the building.'

'The piano?' Amy sounded incredulous. 'Agnes?' She had no idea the boarding house's oldest cleaning lady could be so useful.

'Sideshow Mel told me,' Niffy explained. 'If you ever need to get anything dodgy out of the house, you leave a note under Mel's pillow. Apparently Agnes heads to Mel's room before we're even out of the door for school, so the Neb never has a chance to get in there first.'

'And what does Agnes get out of it?'

'Some very nice Christmas presents, apparently.'

'I still can't believe you and Gina went to Charlie's last night,' Amy said. 'Was it worth it?'

'Hmmm . . . well . . .' Niffy still wasn't sure how she was going to break the Jason news to Amy.

Or *if* she was going to break the Jason news to Amy.

The Year Four sitting room was unusually quiet. Only Gina was in there, reading – to the astonishment of everyone, including Gina – one of her history course books.

'What on earth are you doing?' Niffy demanded as she walked over to the piano, flipped open the lid and reached deep inside to stack beer bottles neatly along the bass end.

'I think it's me who should be asking that question,' Gina replied.

'Temporary storage, out of the Neb's way,' Niffy explained. 'It'll be off our hands by tomorrow. So what's with the history swotting?'

'In case you've forgotten,' Gina began, 'my mother and I had a deal. I only get to go back to California when all my grades are good, and lovely though you are—'

'OK,' Amy interrupted, 'but you have to put that book down now' – she settled herself down on the chair next to Gina's – 'because I'm going to need your help. I'm going to need everybody's help.'

'Oh yeah?' Niffy asked, replacing the piano lid carefully. 'What's the big problem today?'

'Well, you know this debating competition?' Amy
began.

Niffy gave an extravagant roll of the eyes.

'Well, it's about private schools, which I thought
was fine because Penny and her second were going to
be against them and Laura and I—'

'Laura's your second?' Niffy interrupted. 'She's
absolutely useless! About as much help as a chocolate
fireguard.'

'Thanks, Nif, that's really supportive,' Amy
snapped. 'Anyway, Miss Greig has decided she wants to
stretch our debating talents . . .'

This produced a snort from Niffy.

'And' – Amy glared at Niffy but carried on – 'she's
decided we're to take the opposite sides.'

Although Amy suddenly looked close to tears as she
made this revelation, Niffy burst out laughing. 'Oh my
Lord!' she said. 'You're absolutely stuffed. You're going
to have to argue against Penny? Against private
schools! You?! And what is your dad going to say about
this?'

'My dad?'

'Yeah.' Niffy nodded.

Amy hadn't thought about this. She'd thought
maybe she'd just leave the whole subject of the

debate out of her twice-weekly catch-up phone calls.

Amy's dad had a complicated past. He'd grown up in a rough part of Glasgow (something she hoped Penny Boswell-Hackett would never find out). He'd left school young and taken a job as a nightclub barman. A few years later he'd become a nightclub manager and now he owned four nightclubs of his own, making him very successful and very wealthy. He put his meteoric rise down to 'working my arse off'.

He was only thirty-six . . . er, yes – because he'd begun Amy's life when he was just nineteen. At the time, Amy's mum had been eighteen and totally uninterested, which meant Amy had been brought up almost entirely by her dad's parents.

The main reason she was at boarding school was to give her grandparents a break and to let her dad go on working almost every night of the week.

Plus, her dad loved St Jude's. He couldn't get over the fact that his girl went there. Photos of her in her school uniform could be found all over his home, his office and even tucked inside his wallet. Would he like her to be arguing against the school, in front of the whole school? Er . . . no. Definitely not.

'I don't think you're being very helpful!' Amy told Niffy defensively. 'Gina goes to a state school in

America! I thought she might have some advice, some useful things to say about it. If you're just going to laugh, you can get lost, Niff!'

'Why did you get into this in the first place?' Niffy asked, throwing herself down on the sitting room's saggy sofa and showing not the slightest intention of getting lost. 'Penny's going to win. She always wins this kind of thing. The only place you and I have any chance of beating Penny is on the hockey pitch or the tennis court. And even that's bloody hard work. She's your classic St Jude's high achiever. She's probably bulimic; she's probably going to cry for weeks, or at least puke her guts out, if even one of her exam results comes back just a straight rather than a starred A. Her dad will cut off her allowance if she doesn't get into Oxford, even though she'll have to do a Scottish law conversion course afterwards to be a judge in Edinburgh – which, let's face it, is the career trajectory she's on. Why take her on, Amy? Do your own thing, ignore her, don't let her interfere with your life.'

'What do you think I should do then? Just give up? Just go in tomorrow and say I'm backing out, I'm too scared to stand up to her?'

'Couldn't you just be ill on the day of the debate?' Niffy suggested.

'Yeah, that would be the Nairn-Bassett approach, wouldn't it? Just flake out . . . why be bothered?'

'Oh, shut up, Amy.' Niffy's face clouded over.

'What's up with you two?'

Min had walked into the sitting room just in time to hear the last of this heated exchange. As Amy and Niffy were now glaring at each other, Min turned to Gina for an explanation.

'Amy's debate with Penny . . .' Gina began. 'She's got to argue against private schools, so she wants our help and Niffy isn't' – her voice dropped – 'being very helpful.'

'Oh, brother.' Min, fresh from the track, still in a sweaty T-shirt and shorts, perched herself on the piano stool. She was just about to put her fingers to the keys when Niffy told her, 'I wouldn't bother playing that today – well, not the bass notes anyway.'

'Why not?' Min asked, but before anyone could reply, the door swung open and Mrs Knebworth was before them.

'Hello! Beautiful afternoon. Why are we all huddled in here with long faces?'

'We're gated,' Niffy reminded her.

'Oh yes, how could I forget?' Mrs Knebworth made an adjustment to her spectacles and glared at Amy. She'd not said a word about the glasses since last night, but the girls were still concerned that some further punishment lay ahead.

'Well, you could still go and sit on the lawn,' the Neb offered, but there were just exasperated sighs in response to this.

'Oh dear,' she said. She looked at Min, perched on the piano stool. 'They need cheering up, don't they? Probably because they missed that party – at Charlie Fotheringham's, wasn't it?'

Further exasperated sighs followed.

'Dear, oh dear. There will be other parties, girls . . . Min, why don't you give us a little tune? Cheer us all up. I haven't heard you play for ages.'

A tune? A little tune? Amy and Gina exchanged deeply worried glances, whereas Niffy seemed to be suppressing a giggle. Amy glared at her, wondering why she always seemed to find the prospect of landing in the deepest do-do absolutely hilarious. As for Min, she was frozen on the stool, terrified the piano would explode if she touched it.

'Well, come on then . . . All those years of piano lessons weren't wasted on you, surely?' There was a frosty edge to the Neb's voice which set alarm bells ringing for Amy. *Maybe somehow the dreadful woman knew? But how could she?*

What had Niffy said? Min tried to recall the words exactly: *not the bass notes*? Her fingers went gingerly to the far right of the keyboard and she began a high-pitched, tinkly little song.

'Nice,' the Neb commented, and went over to stand so close to the piano that Amy was convinced she'd be able to smell the beer.

Min fingers were flying along the top keys with more confidence now that nothing seemed to be wrong. Then, with a tinkling cadence, she descended the scale towards the grand finale. One chord, then another . . . she was in the middle of the keyboard – Amy and Gina held their breaths – then she finally reached the very end of the tune and – *clump, clump, clump* – hit a note which didn't sound.

Clump, clump – she struck at it again in confusion.

The Neb turned to the piano and Amy shut her eyes, waiting for the sound of the lid lifting.

Mrs Knebworth put out a finger and hit the note: *clump, clump*.

'The hammer isn't hitting the string,' was her verdict.

Her fingers were on the piano lid.

Gina pulled herself into a ball, waiting for the axe to fall.

The housemistress raised the lid a centimetre but then Niffy blurted out: 'A wasps' nest!'

She was standing at the window, pointing. It was the only thing she'd been able to think of in the stress of the situation.

'Where?' Mrs Knebworth let the piano lid fall and hurried over to stand beside Niffy.

'I've just seen five wasps go into that crack underneath the gutter, just there . . .' Niffy was pointing to a spot as high up as possible.

'Oh . . . right,' Mrs Knebworth said, looking up. Not agreeing, because she couldn't see a single wasp; not disagreeing because, as Niffy had suspected, maybe her eyesight wasn't up to the job.

'Well, I'd better book in the handyman and the piano tuner for this week . . .' she said. 'Must put that in the diary.'

And with that, the Neb bustled out of the room to go and write it down straight away.

Before anyone could even let out a breath of relief, a Year Five girl appeared at the doorway with the words: 'Is Gina Peterson in here? Oh, there you are . . . Your mum's on the phone, says it's urgent.'

Chapter Eighteen

'Sadly, we are going to be missing French this afternoon,' Niffy informed Gina during Wednesday's lunch break.

'Are we?' Gina was surprised.

'Yeah . . . I have inside information that between one forty-five and three, Banshee Bannerman is going to be talking to the governors over lunch in the annex and bringing her trusty right-hand woman, Mrs Henderson, along with her,' Niffy announced.

'Huh?' Gina was now even more confused.

'Well,' Niffy went on, 'you remember what Miss Ballantyne said to you this morning?'

How could Gina forget? Miss Ballantyne had handed back her latest history essay with the words: 'Beginning to show signs of improvement, Gina. Maybe you will not be following in your mother's footsteps after all.'

When Gina had asked, 'When are you going to tell me what you mean about my mother, Miss Ballantyne?' the old bat had merely arched her eyebrows and answered, 'Dear, dear, surely that's a question for your mother, not for me.'

Gina had tried asking her mother about Miss Ballantyne's earlier remarks on Sunday, but she hadn't got anywhere.

'I don't remember a history teacher called Miss Ballantyne,' Lorelei had said. 'You asked me about her before. What's she trying to say? That I wasn't a good pupil? She must be thinking about someone else. I always got straight As, Gina. I considered a B a total failure. But how is your work coming along?' she'd wanted to know. 'That's much more important. My school career was over years ago.'

'Why is this phone call urgent, by the way?' Gina had asked. 'The girl who answered the phone said it was urgent. I was really worried.'

'Oh . . . I thought that would make them look for you a bit quicker,' Lorelei had explained. 'It always takes them ages to find you.'

'I'm up on the third—'

But her mother hadn't waited to hear the full story. She'd interrupted with: 'You know what, honey? I'm going to have to ring you back . . . I have another call coming in.'

As she replaced the receiver, Gina had realized that sometimes she didn't miss her mother so much. Sometimes she wished there was something even wider than the Atlantic Ocean between them.

'Do you know what's kept in the locked office behind the Banshee's?' Niffy asked Gina now.

Gina shook her head.

'Files and files and files on every pupil who's ever been at St J's,' Niffy revealed. 'Believe me, I've had a rifle through them before. It's very interesting. All you need is a surname and a leaving date, then you can look up everything about whoever you're interested in. And I think we're all agreed that the Lorelei Winkelmann file has got to be one worth sneaking a peek at.'

For a moment Gina weighed up the risks of being caught in the headmistress's office against the possibility of looking through her mother's school file. There was no difficult decision to be made. She had to see that file. What if there was a really big surprise in there? What if her mother wasn't a straight-A student at all? What if she'd invented that to make Gina feel bad and work harder at school? What if there were B grades in there? Or even *Cs*?

'OK,' Gina told Niffy nervously. 'I think we should go in. But what do we tell Madame Bensimon?'

'Good girl!' Niffy's face broke into a grin. 'I didn't think I'd have to persuade you. I've already prepped Amy to inform Madame that we're both headed to the dentist's this afternoon. Fingers crossed she won't check it with anyone. Now all we need to do is hide in the cloakroom beside the Banshee's office until ten minutes after the bell.'

It was very quiet in the corridors once the rest of the St Jude's girls were all settled into their first lesson of the afternoon. Deathly quiet.

Niffy went first on rubber-soled ballet pumps that were completely noiseless. Gina followed behind nervously, careful to walk on the balls of her feet so that her higher heels didn't clack against the stone floor.

Down the wood-panelled side corridor they went, past the entrance to Mrs Henderson's office and straight to the door with the brass plaque announcing: HEADMISTRESS.

Niffy tapped quietly on the wood – 'Just in case,' she whispered, 'there's been a change of plan.'

There was no reply.

Gina looked at Niffy nervously. What if there was a change of plan in about ten minutes' time and the Banshee appeared when they had their fingers in the files? She didn't feel nearly as trusting of Niffy now; now that her mouth was dry, her hands were shaking and her heart was pounding like a criminal's.

Niffy took the round brass handle in her hands and turned it. The door opened and the two girls stepped inside.

'What are you doing?!' Gina asked in a shocked whisper as Niffy went straight over to the head-mistress's desk and opened a small drawer on the left-hand side.

'Getting the key,' Niffy whispered back. 'I told you. I've done this before . . . just hope she hasn't moved it.'

After a moment of rummaging, she held up a little brass key in triumph. 'Ta-da!'

There was a door in the back wall of the Banshee's office, and this is where Niffy fitted the key into the lock and turned. The door opened and Gina followed her friend into a surprisingly spacious room, bigger than the office, furnished entirely with grey metal filing cabinets.

'Right, it's nineteen eighty-two, isn't it?' Niffy asked,

scanning the neat labels. 'And W for Winkelmann. Let's see . . . let's see . . . Nineteen fifty-two, nineteen fifty-four – maybe into the corner a bit further . . .'

Niffy and Gina couldn't know that things weren't going smoothly at the governors' lunch. The creative arts were the subject of the afternoon's discussion. A vibrant new art teacher and a new head of drama had been installed a year ago, and although the girls were very happy with the teachers, parents were grumbling about 'results'.

Mrs Bannerman claimed that results in art and drama were as healthy as they'd ever been, but one of the governors was arguing that there had been a two per cent drop in As.

'Mrs Henderson?' Mrs Bannerman turned to her assistant. 'I know you looked the past three years' results out for me and put them on my desk, where I'm afraid I've left them . . . Would you mind terribly?' She gave a little smile. 'I just think it would be easier if we had them right in front of us in black and white.'

'Here it is!' Gina exclaimed. 'Nineteen eighty-two!' She pulled open the heavy metal drawer and looked at the neatly alphabetical files in front of her. Her hands went immediately to the 'W'. Walker, Walker, Williams, Winkelmann. 'I've got it!' she whispered to Niffy. 'I've got her file!'

She pulled out the cardboard document case and was surprised to find just three flimsy sheets of paper inside. Was that it? Her mother's entire St Jude's career summed up in three sheets?

Niffy was by her side, peering over her shoulder at the first page. 'That's a copy of her A-level results,' she explained.

Three subjects were listed on the page: mathematics, physics and German.

Gina ran her finger down the results and felt a slight pang of disappointment. 'A, A and A,' she said. 'No big surprise here then.'

'What's on the page behind then?' Niffy asked. 'It should have her standard grades. O-levels they were back then, I think.'

Gina turned over to reveal a row of eight subjects: mathematics, arithmetic, English, French, history, German, physics and biology. The big shock was the row of results: Bs, Cs, one lone A for German and, astonishingly, two Fs!

'She failed two O-levels!' Niffy's surprise was evident. 'History and chemistry! Look!' She was pointing at the page. 'No wonder Miss Ballantyne still goes on about it. St Jude's girls never fail! Not even in the eighties! Blimey, that is shocking! What on earth was she doing? I told you she had white hair and eyeliner and was too cool for school.'

If Niffy was surprised, Gina was shocked. The blood drained from her head, the file in her hands was visibly shaking and tears were springing to her eyes: all she could think about was that her mother had lied to her. Lorelei had always told her what a brilliant straight-A pupil she'd been at school. And right here was the evidence that her mother had lied. *Lied!* And Gina had no idea why.

'What's the other paper behind this one?' Niffy asked.

Gina, blinking hard, turned over the second page of results to find a typed letter, yellowed with age.

Both girls scanned quickly through it.

It was from Jan Winkelmann, Lorelei's father, requesting that his daughter be considered for a place in the Upper Sixth to sit her A-levels.

She has re-taken all her O-levels and achieved outstanding marks. She has already begun her A-level courses and is showing great promise.

All she wishes is to be returned to the school so she can study alongside her St Jude's friends for this final, vital year.

Obviously the distressing matter of her O-levels year is long behind her now.

'Oh my God!' Gina whispered. Here was another thing she didn't know about her mother.

'She hasn't told you anything about this, has she?' Niffy asked, although from the shocked look on her friend's face the answer to this was obvious.

Gina shook her head. She could not believe it. Hadn't her mother said on Sunday: *I always got straight As, Gina. I considered a B a failure?* She closed the file wordlessly, put it back and pushed the drawer shut.

'You're not to tell anyone about this,' Gina insisted, fixing Niffy with a look of deadly seriousness. 'No one. OK?'

Niffy nodded her agreement, and that's when both girls heard the heavy wooden door to the Banshee's office open.

'Uh-oh!' Niffy said under her breath and dropped to her haunches. 'Get out there, Gina, you'll be fine – play the Yank card.'

Gina looked at Niffy in utter incomprehension, but Niffy was waving her frantically towards the door.

Mrs Henderson was just wondering why the door to the records room was open and heading over to check what was going on in there, when a blonde girl walked out with a look of confusion across her face.

'Oh! Hello – maybe you can help me? I'm so totally lost,' the girl asked in a strong American accent, her face breaking into a pleasant smile.

'Oh!' was Mrs Henderson's first response. This must be the Californian girl; she'd not come across her before. 'And where are you supposed to be?' she asked her in brisk Morningside. 'I don't expect to run into pupils wandering aimlessly about the headmistress's office.'

'I've been sent to the staff room,' the girl explained. 'I just seem to have got the directions completely confused.'

When Mrs Henderson began an explanation of how to find the staff room, Gina asked politely, 'Do you think you could just point me in the right direction? It's so confusing out there – so many corridors!' in her best imitation of West Coast ditz.

Back in the head's office, Mrs Henderson picked up

the three pages of printout from Mrs Bannerman's desk, then, catching sight of the key dangling in the lock to the filing room, she shut the door, locked it and replaced the key in Mrs Bannerman's desk drawer. Then she went out of the room and headed back to the governors' lunch.

There were only two words Niffy could think of to express her feelings when she heard the filing-room door close and the key turn in the lock: 'Oh *bum*!'

Squatting down on the floor, she waited until all sounds of Mrs Henderson had disappeared, then looked around the room for a possible means of escape. Well, she couldn't stay here, could she? It might be days before the Banshee thought to look in her records room . . . And there was no point waiting for Gina to rescue her. Gina would be far too scared to do anything on her own.

No, Niffy had to hope that the small sash window, a good metre and a half off the ground, had not been painted shut.

She hoisted herself up onto the filing cabinet closest to the window and began to tug at the stiff catch. It took a few minutes to work it free, but finally she'd managed to force it aside. Now to try the window. She pulled hard at the bottom frame, trying to slide it up. There was some movement – it had not been painted irredeemably shut – but it was very stiff.

After heaving for long enough to make her break into a light sweat, she'd only managed to open it ten centimetres or so, not nearly enough to get out.

She glanced at her watch: it was already 2.45 p.m. Bannerman's lunch was scheduled to end at three. The thought of this gave Niffy enough strength to wrench at the window frame one more time. It opened just a bit further, giving her a gap about thirty centimetres high, forty wide. Enough surely?

She stuck out her head and began to wriggle and squeeze her shoulders through. Now she could see the problems facing her on the other side. Because the school was built on a slope with a substantial basement, although the window was only a metre and a half off the ground on the inside, it was over two metres up on the outside. Below it was a floral border with some softer, fall-breaking plants and some decidedly sharp and jaggy-looking rose bushes.

The window was small and there was no ledge, so Niffy knew she was going to have to dive out head first.

'Big fluffy bum,' she muttered, trying to tell herself that at least the earth looked as if it had been freshly dug. Nif knew from long experience of various daring physical scrapes that it was best not to think about the risks too long. Best just to take a deep breath, hope for a happy ending and get on with it.

So, using her hands to launch herself through the window, she scraped and wriggled out, then fell much faster than she'd intended.

Hands out in front to save herself, she headed for the ground, landing in a clumsy somersault which left her in a heap, momentarily dizzy and winded.

As she lay with her head in the soil, she registered that nothing felt worse than bruised and pricked: she seemed to have got away with it. Picking herself up slowly, she brushed the earth, leaves and prickles from her uniform and prepared to leave the scene of the crime as quickly as possible.

Suddenly Niffy heard voices approaching, but before she had time to register whose voices and where they could be coming from, Mrs Bannerman and Mrs Henderson walked briskly round the corner, leading a posse of governors on an inspection of the grounds.

'Luella Nairn-Bassett,' Mrs Bannerman shot out without hesitation. She prided herself on knowing the full name, age and details of every one of her 443 pupils. 'What on earth are you doing?'

Niffy smiled, looked quickly around the herbaceous border for inspiration and decided on: 'I'm collecting larvae for biology, Mrs Bannerman . . . I thought the best place to try would be the rose bushes.'

Mrs Bannerman stared hard at Niffy. Niffy suspected that Mrs Bannerman's knowledge of the school timetable was so intimate that she would tell her firmly: *But Year Four does not have a biology slot at 2 p.m. on Wednesdays; you, Luella Nairn-Bassett, are supposed to be with Madame Bensimon studying French.*

Mrs Bannerman stared a little longer, then said simply, 'I see. Well, on your way, Luella.'

Niffy would have been delighted to go on her way, but there was a slight problem. In the fall, one of her slip-ons seemed to have slipped off. Her eyes were scanning the ground, frantically trying to locate it.

'Erm . . . I'm actually just waiting for someone else to come round with . . . erm . . . a container. I was supposed to look for the larvae and they're bringing a jar to scrape them into,' Niffy managed.

Mrs Bannerman gave an irritated sigh. Her suspicions were aroused now, but she didn't want the governors to listen to any more of this.

'I see,' she repeated huffily. 'Well, I look forward to

hearing more about this unusual experiment from Mrs MacDuff.'

And with that, she continued on her way, sweeping the governors and Mrs Henderson along with her. Although one of the governors turned to look back at her suspiciously, Niffy dropped to a squat and began hunting for her shoe in earnest.

After a thorough search of the soil, the rose bushes, the entire border and even the surrounding path, Niffy was forced to admit that there was only one obvious place the ballet pump and its incriminating name label could be: on the floor of Banshee Bannerman's records office.

Chapter Nineteen

On Fridays, Amy stayed on for an extra hour at school because of Art Club, so she was walking back to the boarding house on her own. Not that this bothered her. It was a warm, sunny afternoon and she was strolling down the path between the high hedge and the tennis courts.

It was slightly surprising to hear a whistle coming from the bushes. Amy carried on walking at a quickened pace. Now she could hear rustling, as if someone was about to burst through the bushes, so she speeded up to a jog, but was stopped in her tracks by the male voice that called out after her.

'Amy! I've been sitting here all afternoon looking for you.'

She swivelled on her heel and there, just five metres or so away from her, dressed in a scruffy version of the St Lennox uniform, was Jason.

'Jason? What are you doing here?' she gasped. Yet again, he'd managed to take her completely by surprise. She'd not heard from him for fifteen days. In that time, she'd sent him four emails *and* a postcard. Then, when Gina had confided to her yesterday about *Mel*, her toes had curled, her cheeks had burned and she'd wished she'd never set eyes on him. Ever.

And now here he was. Popping out of bushes. Completely unpredictable. And she couldn't control the smile spreading across her face at the sight of him.

'Waiting to see you,' he replied, as if crouching in a hedge for an hour or so was the most obvious way to arrange a meeting.

'Why?' was the question that sprang to Amy's mind.

Jason looked down at the ground, scraped the front of his shoe across the gravel and for a moment or two looked almost shy.

'Well . . . you know,' he began, 'I've been thinking about you. I've missed you.'

So . . . despite the four unanswered emails and postcard . . . Jason Hernandez had been *thinking* of her? Jason Hernandez had *missed* her? Then, to recap: Jason Hernandez seemed to have some actual feelings about her, Amy McCorquodale. Internally, Amy was leaping about in a victory dance; she was running barefoot through grass, rolling crazily down a hill. Externally, she managed to pull the smile off her face and look at him just a little huffily.

Meanwhile Jason pushed a hand through his hair, cleared his throat a little, then shot her one of his smiles. 'C'mon,' he said, walking towards her. 'Haven't you missed me too? Just a little bit?'

Amy's heart, very inconveniently, seemed to have jumped up and lodged itself in her throat, where it was beating wildly and making any chance of saying anything back extremely unlikely.

'Erghmnm . . .' was the sort of strangled sound she managed.

He was smiling. Smiling and approaching. Smiling, approaching and holding out his arms. 'You're very sweet,' he said as he got up close. He was very close, then he was right beside her – in fact, definitely too close for a casual conversation.

'Nmmngh . . .' she said as she realized he was about to put his arms round her and smack her on the lips.

Then she was scrunched up tightly against him and his warm, coffee-flavoured mouth was on hers.

She found herself closing her eyes, wrapping her arms up and over his neck and then, without any intention on her part, she was up on her tiptoes, pressing close to him.

His tongue was sliding against hers and Amy could feel the tingle from the nape of her neck right down to the soles of her feet. If she hadn't had her arms tightly around Jason, she felt her knees might have buckled.

He broke the kiss off only to murmur, 'You're nice,' right into her ear, and then the smooch started all over again.

She clung on, gradually becoming aware of the ache in her jaw muscles. But she didn't want this to end. Not ever.

His hands had slipped down so that he was pulling her hips tightly against his. Amy wasn't so far gone that she missed the effect this was having on Jason.

Oh my God! I am snogging! In the school grounds! With Jason! On the school path! And he is so into it!

And then she thought of Mel.

She didn't mean to think of Mel; in fact she definitely *didn't* want to think of Mel. At all.

Mel's violet eyes, Mel's tarty eyeliner, Mel's bleached hair. Mel's hand in Jason's trousers. Well, that's apparently where it had been. According to Gina. Jason's hand on Mel's boobs. Jason snuggled up in bed with Gina.

Amy suddenly pulled her head back from the kiss, causing it to end with an abrupt smacking sound.

She took a long look at Jason's handsome face. He was gorgeous. She had thought about this face, this mouth, these lips for weeks . . . months!

He tried to smile but the expression now looked a lot more like a smirk. 'I really like you, Amy,' he said.

But his fingers were probably crossed behind his back, weren't they?

Their lips were in contact again: this was going to be hard, Amy realized. But it was obvious he was an untrustworthy louse. It was obvious she should not be kissing him. Or even speaking to him. She had to break this off right now. But, ha . . . here was the catch. He kissed . . . he kissed like . . . heaven. She could feel the brush of his long, soft eyelashes against her cheek.

'Jason . . .' She pulled out of the kiss again and found her voice. 'Jason!' She removed her arms from his neck. 'Go away, Jason!' she managed with a wobble, then added, despite the hurt look on his face, 'I don't want to go out with you!'

She was mortified to hear something closely resembling a sob breaking through those final words.

That was it. She was finished here. All she had to do now was turn on her heel and make a run for it. But as she turned, something caught her eye and held her transfixed to the spot.

It was the hideous vision of Mrs Knebworth storming down the path towards them. There was an expression of absolute fury on her face, and in her hand was a shoe. Despite her rising panic, Amy recognized the shoe. It was Niffy's.

Chapter Twenty

'I am astonished at your behaviour! I am utterly, utterly mortified. By both of you . . . What has got into you? What exactly were you thinking of!'

Mrs Knebworth angry was an unattractive sight. She was flushed, her chins wobbled, her beady little eyes glared. This rant had been going on for about five minutes now and she had worked herself up into a fury.

'I am writing to your parents,' she went on. 'This evening! Have you got any sort of explanation for what has happened? Luella? How did your shoe get into Mrs Bannerman's records office? At least have the decency to try and explain.'

Niffy had been racking her brains ever since she'd had the summons to go to Mrs Knebworth's private sitting room straight away. But no excuse had so far come to mind.

'I can't really say . . .' was all she told the housemistress.

'I see!' Mrs Knebworth stormed. 'Well, you're gated. You'll also go and see Mrs Bannerman first thing on Monday morning. She didn't have time to deal with you this afternoon.'

Then it was Amy's turn to face the two barrels of the Neb's anger.

'To find you behaving like that in the school grounds! It is just beyond belief. Absolutely beyond belief! How long has this been going on?'

'Nothing's been going on. He just appeared out of nowhere – I didn't know—'

'Don't be ridiculous,' the Neb raged. 'Boys don't just pop out of bushes and start kissing you. This was pre-arranged.'

'It wasn't!' Amy argued back, but that just inflamed Mrs K all the more.

'Be quiet! What kind of an idiot do you think I am?'

The snippy reply which sprang to Amy's mind – *A size twenty-four one!* – fortunately stayed there.

'You are gated and your father gets a letter from me. Now off you go to your dorm straight away,' the Neb instructed.

* * *

'That woman is so totally unreasonable!' Amy stormed, once she was back in the dorm with Niffy. 'Letters! Letters? How Victorian is that? Just because she doesn't want to phone and have an actual conversation with my dad. Jason *did* appear from the bushes completely unexpectedly. And . . . I told him to get lost.'

'But you snogged him first?' Niffy wanted to get this straight.

Amy treated her to a furious glare. 'And what were you doing in the Banshee's office?' she asked.

Niffy refused to explain. If she wasn't going to tell the Neb or the Banshee, then she wasn't going to tell Amy either. If anyone should explain anything, it was Gina. But so far, Gina had maintained a total silence. 'And don't feel you have to say anything,' Niffy had told her. 'This is private stuff. Absolutely nothing to do with them.'

'What about the Freedom of Information Act?' she shot back at Amy now.

Amy snorted.

'We should be allowed to see these things,' Niffy argued. 'Anyone would think I'd broken into MI5 or something.'

'I'm going to get Mrs bloody Knebworth back,' Amy

promised. 'I am *so* going to get her back. It's Sports Day next week, isn't it?'

Min issued a groan from behind the book she was reading on her bed.

'Sports Day should be an excellent opportunity to nobble the Neb. What have you got to say about all this anyway, Min? I forgot you were here, you're so bloody quiet.'

'Leave me out of it,' Min instructed. 'Be grateful you didn't have to spring-clean the sitting room. That was my punishment for *stealing her spectacles*.' She looked at Amy significantly. 'I've got enough to worry about. I can't worry about your latest prank as well as everything else.'

'But it wasn't my fault!' Amy insisted. 'At least get that straight.'

'Oh, whatever.' Min pulled the book, *Advanced Level Physics: the Basics*, back up to cover her face.

'I can't even think about this!' Amy wailed. 'I've got to sort out my speech for the debate. It's only nine days away . . . I've written about forty words and they're all rubbish!'

Niffy let out a long sigh at this information before the door opened and Gina came in.

'We're gated,' Amy and Niffy announced together.

'Amy can't be gated for this evening though. The special viewing at the Arts Institute, which you have to go and see for your project?' Gina reminded her. 'And I'm coming with you.'

'Oh yes . . .' Amy had forgotten. 'Do you think she'll still let us?'

'If it's for a project, she'll have to let you.' Niffy didn't sound sure. 'But she'll be furious!'

'And who's to know if we drop in on the Arts Café while we're there?' Gina asked, sounding a little mysterious.

'I can't go to the café. I'll have a quick look round the show and then I've got to do my speech,' Amy moaned.

'But I've been thinking about that: what you need is Dermot,' Gina told her.

'Dermot?' Amy sounded confused.

'Dermot is perfect,' Gina said.

'Didn't know you felt like that about him,' Niffy snapped.

Gina coloured up a little but insisted, 'No! Duh! We need Dermot to help Amy with her speech.'

There was a pause before Amy finally got it. 'Dermot? Oh my God. Dermot!'

Dermot was definitely a comprehensive school guy

who clearly hated private school types – apart from them, of course. He'd have plenty to say on the subject.

'Min, are you going to come with us – provided we're allowed to go, obviously?' Gina asked.

'No. Got to go out and train,' Min replied. She snapped the textbook shut and heaved herself wearily from the bed.

'Girls! I've been counting the hours! What can I get for you?' was Dermot's cheerful greeting as Amy and Gina settled themselves into their favourite sofa after a very quick tour of the gallery downstairs.

'None of those posh nobs joining you today then?' he added.

'No, you're safe,' Amy told him.

'You look smart,' Gina said with a smile. 'New shirt?'

Dermot was dressed in a sky-blue shirt, crisply ironed and tucked into baggy blue jeans. His white waiter's apron was tied round his waist. The shirt, so much better than the thin white nipple-revealers he usually wore, matched his blue eyes, which Gina, not for the first time, found herself drawn towards.

'New uniform,' Dermot replied with a touch of

pride. 'We're shooting upmarket in here. Blue shirts, blue trays, blue mugs . . . so long as they don't start making any blue food or blue coffees, we'll be fine.'

'We want to talk to you about something. You're not too busy, are you?' Gina asked, with a glance around the room, which wasn't nearly as packed as it was on a Saturday.

Dermot perched himself on the arm of the sofa closest to Gina. 'I am never, never, ever too busy to talk to the Daffodils.' He grinned at them.

'Bet you say that to all the girls,' Gina teased.

'No, I don't!' he insisted. 'How many other Daffodils do I know? How many other girls have midnight feasts in long white nighties?'

Gina smacked his arm.

'Oh no, I've upset the vicious one!' he teased, smiling.

When she smiled back at him, he held her look and flushed slightly, which gave Gina an unexpectedly strange, nervy feeling.

'OK.' Amy opened up her notebook and took the lid off her pen in preparation. 'We want you to tell us why you think private schools are a really bad idea and why comprehensives are much better.'

'What? Why?' Dermot exclaimed. 'That's just a wee

bit heavy, isn't it, for a sunny Friday evening? And who says that's what I think, anyway?'

'Oh, come on!' Amy fired back. 'You hate the boys we meet in here – you just called them posh nobs and I've seen you try to pour coffee into their laps.'

'That's because they're tossers,' Dermot insisted. 'Nothing to do with the school they go to.'

'Oh really?' Amy teased.

'Why are you asking me about this anyway?' Dermot wanted to know.

'C'mon, sit down beside us,' Gina urged. 'The boss isn't looking!'

Once they had explained all about the debate and the loathsome Penny and how she had to be defeated, no matter what, Dermot was much more sympathetic.

'Right then,' he began, rolling up his sleeves for emphasis. 'Where do I begin?'

Prompted only by the odd question here and there, Dermot was soon letting rip full throttle: unfairness, elitism, snobbery . . . money buying good exam results.

Amy and Gina couldn't help but be impressed. They'd hoped for a few little pointers, not for the full speech.

'And then,' Dermot added, hardly pausing for

breath, 'let's not forget about how much pressure you're under to perform. Do either of you study subjects you enjoy? Or get any enjoyment out of your studies?'

When they looked at him as if he'd finally lost the plot, he said, 'I didn't think so. At your school it's just about exam results, league tables and a nice long row of As. I mean, don't get me wrong, my school's no picnic. In fact, I'd say it's pretty rubbish, but at least I'm not going to be taken out the back and shot if I don't get starred As in my Highers.'

This made the girls laugh, but it also made Gina think of her mom, who had O-level results she'd not even been able to confess to her own daughter. Gina knew she had to have a conversation with her mother about this, but she still didn't know how to start it.

'But if we suddenly turned up at your school, we'd get our heads kicked in,' Amy insisted.

'Nah! Well . . . you'd get teased for a bit, but you'd soon learn how to blend in,' Dermot said. 'And don't you think that would be a good skill? Their lordships could certainly learn a bit about how to fit in and rub along. And you know what? I don't think it's right that there's no one rich and no one really clever at my school – apart from me, obviously' – he smiled – 'because it would be better for us if there was. We're all under the impression that everyone at private school is a spoiled, swotty tosser.'

Amy laughed.

'You know my dad owns this café,' Dermot told them. 'Well, he was always on at me to try for a scholarship to St Lennox or somewhere like that. "We can just about scrape enough together for it," he'd tell me. But I didn't think it was fair. There are a couple of decent teachers at my school and they need my good results to make sure the headmaster knows they can actually teach. If I'd left to go somewhere else like loads of smart kids did for the sixth form, those teachers would have been left with the dregs and a long list of Ds, Es and Fs.

'I study on my own,' he added. 'No one comes at me with a big stick like at your place. I'm an independent thinker. So there! If my grades are good enough, I'm going to go to Edinburgh University. But I'll have to work here for a year first to get the money together.'

Gina looked at Dermot with fresh admiration after this speech. Meanwhile Amy was scribbling hard in her notebook.

'Look at you! It's Friday and you're still swotting –

that's why I'd never go out with a St Jude's girl!' he teased.

Amy looked up from her notes and couldn't resist asking him, 'Have you got a girlfriend, Dermot?'

At this, Gina found herself staring at the ice cubes floating in her glass of Coke, but she realized she was listening very hard. She was much more intensely interested in Dermot's answer than she would like to have admitted to anyone. Including herself.

'Nah,' he said casually.

Gina suddenly felt light-headed.

'Not really . . .' he added.

And now Gina felt as heavy as a lump of stone.

'What's that supposed to mean?' Amy asked him straight back.

'Oh, you know . . .' Dermot got up from the sofa he'd perched on, suddenly keen to escape this line of questioning. 'There's this girl and . . .'

'She doesn't like you?' Amy persevered.

'Who knows?' He gave a small smile and held his tray protectively up over his chest. 'Female of the species . . .'

'You should ask her!' Amy encouraged him.

'Yeah, right . . . thanks! I hadn't thought of that!'

Before he turned to head back to the bar, Dermot's

eyes met Gina's briefly, and once again that feeling shot through her. This time she could feel the warm prickling of a blush starting up at her collarbone. She took a gulp of Coke to cool herself down.

Gagged. Choked. Spluttered. Coughed dramatically. Turned a dangerous shade of red.

'You should have had a coffee,' Amy told her.

Chapter Twenty-One

'*Min!*' Amy burst into the study room (where else would Min be at five on a Saturday?) and announced, 'There's someone here to see you!'

'What? Me?' Min was astonished. 'But I'm not expecting anyone! I can't even think who it could be!'

'Come on!' Amy insisted. 'This is someone I've invited for you. Don't worry,' she added, seeing the anxious look on Min's face. 'You're going to be just as pleased to see her as she will be to see you. And I've told her all about the biology thing and your parents and the doctor business and we've had a few ideas. But come on, Min, for goodness' sake. She's already waiting for you in the Year Four sitting room.'

'What?' Min repeated, totally mystified, but getting up from her seat. 'The biology thing?'

As Amy held open the sitting-room door, she

watched with pleasure as Min's face turned from confused to surprised to utterly delighted.

'Mrs Wilson!' she cried. 'What are *you* doing here?'

'Come to sort you out, my dear,' replied the physics teacher, who'd been happy to be summoned from her leave of absence, nursing her husband, to come to the aid of her most promising pupil. 'I think you owe your friend Amy a big thank you. She's been worrying herself silly about you,' she went on, smoothing out her tweedy skirt and settling herself down on one of the sitting-room chairs. 'Sit,' she instructed, patting at the seat next to hers.

'Now what is all this fuss and fret I've been hearing about? Of course you're not going to sit a biology A-level, Asimina!' Mrs Wilson said briskly. 'What a waste of your precious, God-given talents that would be. I think it's obvious you should be considering physics, mathematics and chemistry.'

'But—'Min began.

'Shh!' her teacher insisted. 'I've not finished yet!'

Although she sounded stern, there was a cheerful smile on her ruddy, forty-something face. 'All these subjects can have a wonderful medical application. Amy and I have been doing some research. There's oncology, the study of cancer – it's full of chemotherapists and radiologists. You could become one of our top medical researchers, Asimina. A biology Higher, rather than an A-level, might be something to tuck under your belt while you're en route to your A-levels. But it's not even strictly necessary.'

Min was finding it hard to keep her mouth from falling open at these words: medical research! Why hadn't she thought about that? Radiology? Chemotherapy? Chemists made medicines . . . physicists developed MRI scanners. If she was a medical researcher, she could be in a lab, not having to deal with live, bleeding patients. She would just need a C, maybe a respectable B in her biology Higher. And she could manage that, even though her mind would be on the higher plains of A-level physics and maths.

'Now, just as soon as you've taken that astonished look off your face, we'll talk it through a little, then why don't I help you make the call and explain it to your parents?' Mrs Wilson asked. 'I thought that might be of use to you.'

Now Min looked close to fainting with surprise.

'Tea!' Amy insisted, holding out a mug to Min. 'There's loads of sugar in it – good for shock.'

'No wallowing like this again, Asimina!' Mrs Wilson scolded, taking the tea offered to her by Amy. 'It's not good for the system. And do your parents know about the fainting and vomiting?'

'Well . . . a bit. But I've not really explained it to them.'

'Well, you must!' Mrs Wilson insisted. 'What use is a doctor who passes out at the sight of blood?'

'Wake up, Nif!' Amy hissed. 'Come on, wakey, wakey. We have work to do!'

Amy was already up, her alarm clock having beeped at 3.30 a.m. Now she just had to wake her accomplices.

'What is it now?' Gina wanted to know.

'We're going down to the kitchen. It's time to get the Neb back.'

When the plan had been explained, Niffy and Gina couldn't help feeling that it was vicious and twisted, but nevertheless a stroke of genius.

The three (because Min would never have agreed to take part in this) crept down the stairs in the dark and headed for the boarding-house kitchen.

In the enormous fridge, they located the items for sabotage. There were five large pots of double cream and six packets of butter.

Mrs Knebworth always laid on a sensational cream tea after Sports Day for the parents of the boarders.

This and the Christmas party were her big show-off moments. She would bake like a demon all day long and be ready by late afternoon, with cream cakes, scones and her legendary strawberry tarts in the summer, chocolate and fruit cakes in the winter.

Because the Neb was always on some sort of diet, she claimed that she never so much as licked a spoon when she was baking, and allowed herself just one sliver of cake at the teas.

'Fingers crossed she's not feeling too greedy to-morrow,' Niffy said as Amy brought out the instruments of cake torture.

In a small plastic bag, she had a tube of extra-strong garlic paste, an onion and a large tub of salt.

'Right, I need teaspoons, a plate, a sharp knife and someone to find the flour and the baking powder,' she instructed.

'Oh! This is bad.' Gina was worried. 'This is *so* bad . . .'

'So bad, it's good!' Niffy giggled mischievously.

The five pots of double cream were carefully part-opened, just enough to allow a teaspoon of garlic paste to be vigorously stirred around inside and removed, so that no trace of the crime remained.

The paper around the butter was opened at the top

so that half an onion could be rubbed across them, then carefully refolded.

Just as Niffy and Gina were bringing out the flour to be liberally dosed with salt, they thought they heard a noise in the corridor and all ducked down under the kitchen table, praying the Neb didn't come in – a table didn't exactly make for a great hiding place.

But whatever the noise had been, it didn't bring anyone into the kitchen.

'Come on, quickly!' Gina instructed, holding open the flour bags so that Amy could tip in the salt, then stir it through.

When everything had been tidied away as carefully and noiselessly as possible, they tiptoed back through the house and upstairs to bed, Amy tucking the paste, onion and salt into her school bag so she could drop them into a bin at school the next day.

Chapter Twenty-Two

St Jude's looked 'glorious' on Sports Day, just as Banshee Bannerman's memo to pupils, staff and groundsmen had instructed.

The freshly cut grass gleamed in the bright July sunshine, the newly painted white windows dazzled, little red and white bunting flags fluttered in the breeze and the table laden with sporting silverware sparkled.

Even the girls, who'd been able to ditch the sludge-green sweatshirts in favour of white shirts or athletics vests because of the warmth, looked much prettier than usual.

As soon as the start of the 800 metres was announced over the crackly tannoy system, Gina, Niffy and Amy joined the other Year Four girls and jostled their way towards the front of the crowd at the finishing line for a good view of Min's race.

'Is she going to be OK?' Gina worried. 'She said her times have been bad for weeks.'

'She's feeling better,' Amy replied confidently.

'I don't know,' Niffy chipped in. 'She's pulled out of the four hundred metres because she wasn't sure if she could manage both races.'

'Trust me' – Amy smiled – 'she's feeling much better now. Mrs Wilson was brilliant – helped to phone her parents and settled the whole doctor problem once and for all. Min will run like the wind.'

'I hope you're right,' Niffy replied, crossing the fingers on both hands and hugging herself for luck.

'How did your long jump go, by the way?' Amy wanted to know.

'Pants, total sandy pants!' Niffy replied, and when Amy pulled a puzzled face, she explained gloomily, 'Did a cracking jump, but fell backwards instead of forwards. Now my pants are full of sand, and Suzannah from Year Five – who can do a Fosbury Flop, by the way, and is going to win the high jump – won.'

'Oh dear . . .' Amy would have added something more sympathetic but the crack of the starting pistol sounded and the six girls taking part in the 800-metre race were away, setting off down the straight in a close group. By the time they rounded the first corner, three had broken away slightly, and the girls could see that Min, with her long hair streaming out behind her, was among the front runners.

'Come on, Min!' Niffy screamed at the top of her voice as the runners tore past them, on their way to completing the first lap.

'Go, Min, go!' Amy shouted above the cries of support for Lucy, Lauren, Willow and the others.

'Louisa's going to do it!'

They all turned at the sound of Penny's voice behind them.

'She's already logged the best time of the term – just watch,' she told them smugly.

Amy dodged quickly through the crowd to get away from Penny, Gina and Niffy on her heels.

'Come on, come on!' Niffy said, but to herself, as Lauren, Louisa and Min began to widen the gap between themselves and the three other runners.

Louisa and Lauren were hugging the inside lane: if Min was going to get past them, she would have to overtake on the outside, losing precious seconds. As they rounded the final bend, Louisa and Lauren began to pull ahead.

'Come on, Min!' Gina shouted, caught up in the race. '*Go, GO!*'

Min launched herself out of the inside lane, pumping her arms and legs like pistons to build up the speed needed to overtake on the outside.

The final 100 metres or so lay ahead of them, and all three girls were racing hard, arms pummelling, lungs fit to burst.

Gina held her breath, terrified that someone was going to trip or stumble, bring Min down by mistake and take this chance away from her.

It was too close: Lauren and Louisa were neck and neck, Min still fractionally behind. But then some unknown power seemed to sweep over Min. In a surge of acceleration, her legs pumped faster, carrying her past the others and over the finishing line a clear metre ahead. But as soon as it was over, she collapsed in a heap onto the ground.

'Min!' Niffy exclaimed. 'Is she OK?'

The three girls rushed towards her, but were held back by one of the PE teachers manning the line.

'Give her a moment,' she instructed.

One of the other teachers Min brought a drinks bottle. She helped her into a sitting position and poured some of the liquid into her mouth.

Min spluttered; she was gasping for breath and

waving the drink away. But the PE teacher was reassuring her and offering another mouthful.

For several long minutes Min's friends watched as she slowly got her breath back, took long restorative mouthfuls of the salt and glucose fluid and finally got up onto her exhausted, wobbly legs.

Only when the tannoy announced, 'The eight hundred metre winners are: first, Asimina Singupta; in second place, Lauren Gaitling; Louisa McKay, third; and we have a new school record,' did a smile spread across Min's face.

'Come on!' Niffy rushed down to the edge of the track as Min wobbled towards them. 'Let's help her get her trophy, then' – exchanging a significant look with Amy – 'it's time for the famous boarding-house tea.'

Gina's stomach suddenly began to churn with worry.

'Oh my God!' Niffy exclaimed. 'There's my mum and dad! No! It can't be. My mum and dad?' she asked, sounding puzzled and pointing at a couple still some distance away across the playing field. 'Is that them?' She shaded her eyes with her hands to get a better look. 'It's just I can't remember the last time I saw them walking along arm in arm. The last time I saw them—' But she broke off because it wasn't a particularly pleasant memory.

What she saw now was a middle-aged couple walking closely together. They were talking and her dad was looking at her mum with kind concern. Niffy could not remember when she'd last seen anything like this between them.

Mr Nairn-Bassett, in his tweed jacket and panama hat, looked every inch the country gent, while Mrs N-B looked quite alarmingly like Niffy. If Niffy wanted to know what she'd look like in her forties, here was the flash forward.

Mrs N-B had the same gangly arms and legs and unruly mop of brown hair, although hers was run through with grey. She was wearing a faded red summer dress which hung a little baggily round her flat chest and skinny frame. Even her sandals seemed large and loose on her feet.

'Mum!' Niffy shouted out finally. 'Dad! I'm over here!'

'Lu, darling!' Mrs N-B came over, wrapped two bony arms round her daughter and hugged her tight. 'And Amy!'

As Niffy hugged her dad hard with a look of unmistakable relief on her face, Amy was treated to Mrs

N-B's embrace and a kiss on each cheek, then Min, then a surprised Gina.

'I've heard so much about you – the Yank!' Mrs N-B told her.

Niffy rolled her eyes and scolded, 'Mum! Look at you, you're so thin! Are you OK?'

'Oh! Don't be silly – just rushing about like a mad thing, as usual,' Mrs N-B replied. 'So, Min, well done. Are we going to watch you get your gong then?'

'I think we'll have to help her up onto the podium,' Amy said. 'She's still so shaky.'

'I'll be fine – just a few more mouthfuls of the magic stuff' – Min waved her drinks bottle at them – 'and I'll be right as rain.'

'You know that saying, "to die trying",' Gina added; 'it's just a saying, Min! You're not supposed to actually kill yourself on the race track.'

The cream tea, laid out across the top table in the dining room, was so perfect, so *English*, so photogenic, it didn't quite look real. It was the kind of spread set out at five-star country house hotels, or for the pages of glossy lifestyle magazines. In short, it looked far too good to actually eat.

Three beautiful Victoria sponge cakes filled with

thick cream and jam, lightly dusted with icing sugar, took centre stage, surrounded on all sides by heaps of raisin-studded scones, fresh from the oven. Then there were platefuls of strawberry tarts, with crisp pastry and crème pâtissière, the perfect pointed berries shiny under a layer of pink glaze.

'Come in,' Mrs Knebworth trilled at the groups of parents and girls filtering in through the big front door. 'Welcome! Straight into the dining room – help yourselves, make yourselves at home.'

Gina, Niffy and Amy all exchanged glances. Mrs Knebworth looked so happy, so proud and pleased with herself.

She was going to *die*! Gina couldn't help thinking. The Neb was going to die of mortification. Her beautiful tea was ruined! She and the others had spoiled the whole thing.

Gina watched in horror as the first parents filed towards the laden table. Slim and elegant mother number one accepted a cup of tea but turned down the offer of a cake. Gina was relieved. Maybe everyone was full . . . Maybe no one would take a salted scone or a slice of garlic cake . . .

'Oh, that looks fantastic, yes please!' The father next in the queue picked up a plate and asked for some cake, then took a tart and squeezed it onto the plate too.

Amy and Niffy were giggling. *How could they?*

'This is going to be terrible,' Gina whispered to them. 'The Neb is going to cry; she's going to be utterly heartbroken.'

'It's too late now,' Amy whispered back. 'Short of rushing up and knocking the table over, what can we do?'

They watched the people crowding round the spread.

Gina really had considered sweeping everything onto the floor by 'accident', but as Amy said, it was too late now.

'Mrs Bannerman!' Niffy hissed, spotting the head-mistress. 'Over there! The Banshee's joining us!'

'Good grief!' Even Amy looked worried now. 'The Neb's humiliation will be complete. Oh dear . . . I wasn't expecting quite so many people . . . I thought it would be a bit more low-key.'

'Let's get out of here,' Niffy suggested.

Gina looked up to see the father who'd already got his food dig his fork into the strawberry tart. As he lifted the first piece towards his mouth, she rushed for the dining-room door.

The three girls stood outside in the hall, waiting for

the sounds of coughing or gagging, the murmurs of complaint to begin.

This was big. This was a big, big mistake. They were going to be in so much trouble. Not for the first time, Gina imagined herself packing her bags and heading home early in disgrace. Not that she was the only one who would have lots of explaining to do – she *still* hadn't said a word to her mother about the mysterious exam results. Lorelei wasn't exactly easy to talk to if you weren't telling her what she wanted to hear.

'Girls!' Mrs Knebworth's head came round the dining-room door. 'What are you doing out here?' she asked sharply.

'Erm . . . well . . .' was all Niffy could manage.

'Come in.' The Neb beckoned. 'Let me sort you out at once!'

Reluctantly, the three headed into the dining room once again. To their surprise, everything seemed astonishingly normal. Parents and girls were sitting at the tables, chatting, drinking tea and . . . eating! Eating happily! Forks were spearing at pieces of cake; the gorgeous strawberry tarts were being devoured greedily.

The three girls sat down at the end of one of the tables, looking at each other uneasily.

'Is everyone being really polite?' Amy wondered.

'Surely not!' Niffy shook her head.

'Maybe we didn't use enough stuff?' Gina asked.

But at the thought of the onion being smeared back and forth across the butter, the garlic paste swirling round the cream, the spoons and spoons of salt, she suspected this could not be the answer.

'Here we are!' Mrs Knebworth set three plates before them with a large slice of cake on each. 'You deserve it!' she trilled.

There was no denying it: the cake looked fantastic. The sponge was light and fluffy, raspberry jam and cream oozed from between the layers.

'It's a mystery then,' Niffy said, picking up the cake with her fingers and preparing to bolt down a big mouthful.

Suddenly Amy and Gina felt ravenously hungry too. They loaded their forks and put substantial pieces into their mouths.

There was a moment's pause; it took a split second for the shock to register. Then the coughing and gagging began.

The salt! The garlic! The disgusting flavours mingled in their mouths with the sponge, cream and jam.

Aaaaaargh! Amy and Gina turned red and attempted to swallow the vile mouthfuls. Niffy unceremoniously spat the offending cake back out onto her plate.

Min arrived at their side, a half-eaten scone laden with cream and jam in her hand. Taking another bite, she said through her mouthful, 'What's up with you lot? This is Mrs K's best spread yet.'

Suddenly the Neb was at their side again, not looking quite so friendly this time. In fact she was frowning and her mouth looked mean and thin.

'I have had to bake the entire tea twice,' she snapped. 'Do you have any idea how much work that involved? Even worse, a great deal of perfectly good food has gone to waste because of you selfish, silly little girls. You are on washing-up duty until the end of term and you will never, ever meddle in my kitchen again,' the Neb declared, before turning, expression set back to welcoming smile, to the parents behind her.

Gina could feel her toes curling in her shoes at these words; Amy hung her head and even Niffy didn't seem to be shaking with the need to giggle.

'I think we should go upstairs,' Amy suggested. Both Gina and Min nodded in agreement but Niffy reminded them that she had her parents to look after.

* * *

'Are Niffy's parents really going to take us all out for dinner?' Min asked, once they were back in the peace and quiet of the dorm.

'That's the plan,' Amy replied. 'They're just having a cup of tea in the sitting room – I think there's something Niffy's mum wants to talk about in private.'

'In private?' Min wondered.

'I know,' Amy said. 'Sounds ominous, doesn't it?'

'Did you know that she thinks her parents are having real problems?' Gina had to ask.

Amy just sighed. 'I think it's been like this for years. But maybe it's got worse lately. She's been worried about them all term – worried there's something going on that they won't tell her about.'

'What are you going to do about Mrs K?' Min asked from her bed, where she was lying flat out, trying not to doze off after her strenuous afternoon.

'Maybe we should buy her a bunch of flowers?' Gina suggested.

'Oh God . . .' The reluctance on Amy's face was obvious. 'Well, yes, I suppose so. Otherwise she'll never, ever let us forget about it.'

'She's not really that bad—' Min began.

'Yes she is!' Amy retorted. 'I've been here since I was

ten and so has Niffy, and we're agreed that the Neb is a daughter of the devil.'

'Well, I've been here since I was thirteen and I really don't think she is!' Min answered back, aware of how childish this argument sounded.

'Have you always shared a dorm with Niffy?' Gina asked Amy to try and change the subject.

'Yeah. There are a few other girls who've been here as long as us, but I've always shared with Nif.'

Just then the door flew open and Niffy burst in. To their surprise, she was streaming with tears and flung herself down on her bed, face first, sobbing noisily.

'Niffy!'

First Amy, then Min and Gina huddled round her bed, patting her on the back and asking what the matter was.

When only sobs came in reply, Amy asked gently, 'Are they getting divorced? Is that what the problem's been?'

The sobbing went on. Long, slow minutes passed with Amy just patting Niffy's back, Gina and Min looking at each other, not sure what to do next.

Finally Niffy was able to blurt out, 'No . . . no . . . I just knew it! I knew all along that something was not right. My mum's just told me that—'

Her sobs broke out anew and she struggled to get the words out. 'My mum's ill. She's known for months and she's only just told me.'

The news was met with a stunned silence.

It took a minute before Amy managed to ask, 'What's the matter with her?'

Niffy gave a horrible strangled gurgle. 'She's got cancer,' she blurted out. 'Some kind of leukaemia, but she says it's not the really serious one. I can't believe there's any other kind!'

The three girls round her bed all looked at each other in fright now.

'Where *is* your mum?' Amy asked when Niffy's sobs seemed to have subsided a little.

'She's still in the sitting room where I left her. I told her not to follow me!' Niffy replied, head still buried in her pillow. 'I have to go home,' she added. 'I mean, I have to leave St Jude's and go to school at home but she doesn't want me to do that! Says she wants my life to carry on as usual . . . *as usual*' – Niffy's voice rose close to a shout – 'as bloody usual, while she goes off and threatens to die on me! And if I don't go home' – she sat up now and wiped hot tears from her cheeks – 'she's going to have to sell Ginger! Because she's not well enough to ride him.'

It was no use, the sobs broke out again but Niffy managed: 'Don't think I'm more upset about Ginger than Mum, it's not that. But I love him Too . . .' And with that Niffy fell face first back onto her bed.

'I want to go home,' were the words that came through the pillow, 'and I really *don't* want to go home!'

Only Amy really understood what her friend meant.

They'd been boarders together for five years. Amy understood perfectly that Niffy didn't want to leave school and have to deal with her family and all its problems full time. There had been moments for Amy when boarding school had been a protective bubble of normality away from her unconventional home life. It would be so hard for Niffy to leave.

The door opened and Mrs N-B entered the room, looking much more composed than her daughter. She greeted the girls with a smile and, standing with her back against the door, told them, 'I'm really sorry about this. I've upset Luella much more than I meant to. I mean . . . she's much more upset than she really needs to be.'

'I'm so sorry about your news.' Amy wanted to make it clear that Niffy had told them.

Mrs N-B sat on the end of Niffy's bed and ran a hand through her daughter's hair. 'It's not nearly as bad as you think, Lu,' she said softly. 'They've got it so early . . . Please don't cry. Please don't cry, Lulu – you'll set me off as well.'

Looking away to give them some privacy, Gina thought how strange it was that there were three different Nairn-Bassett girls: Luella belonged to the school, Lulu belonged to her family; Niffy was theirs.

'I want to come home, Mum. Just for a term or two,' came from the pillow. 'You've got to let me. Just to make sure you're really going to be OK.'

'Don't be silly,' Mrs Nairn-Bassett soothed. 'Think how much you'd miss your friends.'

Amy, Min and Gina all looked at each other. They knew they had to help Niffy. If she was in no fit state to fight her corner with her mother today, then they would have to do it for her.

'Mrs N-B . . .' began Min, who now had some experience of difficult conversations with parents.

Chapter Twenty-Three

'Doesn't everyone deserve a fair start? A fair chance at making the best of their life?' Amy took a deep breath before she went on, trying not to let the piece of paper in her hands wobble too much. 'Why should someone who lives in the wrong part of town not be able to go to a good school? Why should someone whose parents can't afford to send them to a school like this miss out on good exam results and the chance of being well qualified for the rest of their life?'

She looked up . . . Oh dear – she definitely wasn't going to do that again. There were far too many faces out there, all staring back at her. Everyone looked deadly serious and grim – it was totally freaking her out.

Before she'd got up to begin her speech, she hadn't felt too nervous, but now that she was coming to the end of it, she was feeling deeply shaken. Her words didn't sound convincing even to her. And the poisonous smiles on the faces of Penny and Louisa over on the other side of the table were hardly reassuring.

'So, to conclude,' Amy ploughed on, 'this house believes in a fair and just system of education for all, not just for the few who can afford to pay for it.'

She sat down abruptly and listened to the applause. There was no doubt that it was a little restrained, a little polite. Oh, capital S, H, I and T. They were going to lose.

Penny stood up with a beaming smile. There were no notes clasped in her hands – she was going to do this from memory, the cow! Look at her fingers! Not the slightest sign of trembling.

With a voice full of confidence, with a positive swagger, Penny kicked off her speech. She was leaning forward; she was really speaking *to* her audience, not at it. She was winning them over, convincing every single one of them. Look! There were smiles and nods of agreement as she rattled on, 'Wealth isn't usually an accident: almost everyone in this room has talented parents who work really hard every day to make the money to send you here. To the best school in Edinburgh—' Loud claps interrupted her words. 'To the best school in Scotland!' She punched the table for emphasis. Louder clapping and a whoop or two followed.

'Your parents want the best for you!' Penny's voice was passionate. 'They didn't want to dump you in some mediocre comprehensive where nobody cares about the best; where "good enough" and "scraping by" are all that is required . . .'

Amy struggled with the desire to bury her head in her hands. Why had she ever thought this would be a good idea? One moment of pomposity as she'd met Penny at the notice board and now, here she was, being humiliated in front of the entire school.

As Penny's speech finished to thunderous applause, Amy wondered how she was going to be able to sit through the two supporting speeches without screaming.

Finally it was time for first Penny and then Amy to give their brief concluding speeches. There was no mistaking the sneer on Penny's face as, completing hers, she sat down to further loud applause. Once she'd made sure Amy was looking, she spread her thumb and forefinger into an L for loser and showed it to her.

Amy looked away in disgust, stood up – and

discovered to her surprise that she'd totally lost her temper and didn't care what anyone in this smug little Penny-loving audience thought of her any more. She put down the page she'd prepared and began to talk off the top of her head.

Suddenly she could only think about her dad, who'd gone to a school so rubbish, he'd left at sixteen without a single qualification, even though he was a bright guy – he still couldn't write a sentence without making at least three mistakes. That just wasn't fair, was it?

'Fine!' she stormed at her audience. 'That's fine. You just sit there smugly and congratulate yourselves on the fantastic results you're all going to get. Fantastic because your parents have bought the best teachers for you; fantastic because the school has weeded out everyone who isn't clever enough, isn't committed enough, isn't even stable enough! It must be a real cushy number teaching here: no one with a problem is allowed to stay on at this school, are they?!'

She was aware of the complete quiet in the room now.

'So all those other kids who leave school at sixteen without a qualification, because they're poor, or badly taught, or ADD or dyslexic, or had no one encouraging them, not even somewhere quiet at home to go and study . . . we'll just forget about them, will we?

'Who cares about them? Not you lot: the lawyers, accountants and doctors of tomorrow. Because you went somewhere else. You haven't got a clue what they've been going through. And they won't be able to change anything when they grow up, because there's no way they'll become lawyers, accountants, doctors or teachers.

'But that's fine. If you're happy with that; if you're happy for this city to have some of the best schools in the country and some of the absolute worst, then that's just fine. You vote for them.' She pointed at Penny and Louisa, then, suddenly feeling a tightness at the back of her throat, sat down abruptly.

After a moment or two of stunned silence, much louder applause than she'd expected broke out.

'Oh, never mind Penny,' Niffy told Amy for about the fiftieth time that day as they walked along the boarding-house corridor after supper. 'Thirty-three people voted for you, didn't they? They can't all have been your friends, because you've only got about three friends! I think this shows incredible promise: a career in the law is calling to you!'

'Oh, put a cork in it!' Amy replied.

'You won!' Niffy reminded her. 'You won! What did Mrs Greig say again? "Provocative but impassioned."'

The payphone in the corridor booth began to ring – an extremely unusual sound: it hardly ever got the chance because there was almost always someone on it.

Neither Niffy nor Amy rushed to answer it, because this would involve running round the boarding house in search of the person the call was for.

'Oh, go on,' Amy instructed Niffy once the fourth ring had sounded.

Niffy reluctantly went over and lifted the receiver. 'Hello? Who? Oh! Yeah . . . That's me . . . Who is this?'

Amy edged in a little closer to her friend to make sure she didn't miss any of the conversation.

'How are you?' Angus was asking Niffy: Angus of the leopard-skin g-string, Angus of the dorm visit, Angus of the cheeky smiles and daring bets.

'I'm fine,' she replied, still sounding surprised. Why on earth was Angus phoning her? Was this some kind of a wind-up?

'I just wondered if you were going to be around . . . you know . . . during the summer?' Angus asked, sounding very unsure of himself.

Around during the summer? Oh! Poor boys! Niffy couldn't help thinking. They were so clueless and kind of hopeless. They should not be the ones who had to ask for dates; really that should be a girl's job. Always.

'Are you asking me out, Angus?' Niffy asked, and Amy began to giggle beside her.

'Well . . . erm' – there was some vigorous throat-clearing going on – 'sort of . . .' Angus concluded.

'That's really sweet of you,' Niffy said, 'but . . . erm . . . I'm not going to be in Edinburgh much. I'm going home to Cumbria and I'll be at a school there for a while because my mum's . . . not very well,' she added.

'Oh,' Angus replied. 'I'm sorry.'

There was a pause while he considered what to say next. 'Don't be too wild then,' he added, and there was such an obvious note of disappointment in his voice that Niffy felt she had to help him out.

'Cumbria is lovely – you should come and visit. You know my brother Finn, don't you?'

'Finn? Yes. Well . . . that would be great. Fantastic. Well, I'll do that! OK, well, great to talk to you. I'll definitely try and do that . . . OK then . . . Well, take care and . . .'

Just as he was about to hang up and possibly punch

the air and do a little victory dance, Niffy had to prompt him: 'Angus?'

'Yeah?'

'Do you want to take my home phone number? That way you can phone me and we can make the arrangement.'

'Oh yes . . . erm . . . just hang on – got to go and find a pen . . . something to write on . . .'

Once Angus was off the line, Niffy couldn't help turning to Amy with an excited giggle.

'So Angus coming to Cumbria is a good thing, is it?' Amy asked.

'I think so!' Niffy answered with a grin.

Then, holding the receiver up so that no one else could call in, she told Amy to go and get Gina.

'Gina? Why?' Amy asked.

'There's something she has to talk to her mum about before she goes back home.'

Chapter Twenty-Four

'Mom, it's Gina. Hi!'

'Oh, hi. Hi, honey. How are you?'

After Gina had caught up with everything going on at home, Lorelei wanted to know all about school and Gina's schoolwork. How was it coming along? Had she finally settled in and got her head down?

'Yeah,' Gina assured her, 'I've been working really hard. My biology results are good. My physics is apparently improving . . .'

'That's great! Fantastic news!'

Gina went on down the list. 'I think even Madame Bensimon might have some hope for me, and English . . .' She thought about Mrs Parker and all her praise and encouragement over the past few weeks – *Another A for Gina . . . Girls, we have an essayist in our midst, a composer of polemics, a future journalist maybe? An opinion former? At the very least, a brilliant book reviewer.* No teacher had ever been so nice to her before, and as a result, her reading list was growing by the day.

'English,' Gina told her mother modestly, 'is going really well. I'm sure I'm going to get a really good report card for this term, Mom. You'll be proud of me. Maybe you'll even let me come home.'

'Wow, baby, I *am* proud of you!' Lorelei replied. 'Of course you're going to come back now! We can't wait to see you. All of us. Your friends included. I was speaking to Paula's mom and Paula's got a whole summer of fun planned out for you. Three parties in the first week of the holidays alone. And you may go!

'It must have been so hard for you,' she finally acknowledged, 'fitting into a totally different school, with all those new people. I am so proud of you.'

'So . . .' Gina took a little breath to help her get the question out. 'Mom . . . how come you did so badly at your O-levels?'

She pressed the receiver tightly against her ear. For a while all she could hear was the gentle buzzing a transatlantic line sometimes makes when no one is talking.

'Oh . . . you found out about that?' Lorelei asked in

a voice which sounded much less certain than usual. 'How did you—?'

'Never mind how I found out,' Gina interrupted. 'I think you should just tell me what happened.'

'But I . . . I didn't want you to find out about that,' Lorelei said.

'Why not?' Gina asked, exasperated. 'In case I thought you were anything less than perfect?'

Down the line, she could hear her mother's deep sigh.

'Don't you think you should have told me about this?' she went on. 'Don't you think just a little bit of information about how you did at school might have been helpful to me?'

There was a pause before Lorelei said in her defence, 'I just wanted to be a really good role model for you.'

'By lying?' Gina shot back. 'That's wonderful – I've learned so much from that!'

'Gina! There are lots of things I've done well' – there was a quaver in Lorelei's voice that Gina didn't think she'd ever heard before – 'but nothing's more important to me than being the best possible mother to you, because . . . well . . . you know . . .'

Gina realized what her mother was trying to say:

until Mick had come into their lives, she had been bringing up Gina all on her own.

Much of the anger had gone out of Gina's voice when she told her mom, 'You *are* the best. But that doesn't mean you have to pretend to be perfect.'

The quiet buzz of transatlantic silence filled Gina's ear again. She worried that her mother was going to cry – something she didn't think she'd ever experienced before. Well, not for a very long time anyway.

'So what happened that year?' Gina heard herself asking, half wanting to know, half dreading upsetting her mother even more.

After a long pause Lorelei said, 'It was a really difficult time. My dad was sick and I met this boy who was there for me when I needed someone.'

'Oh.' It suddenly dawned on Gina that she didn't know anything about her mother's first boyfriends . . . had never thought to ask about them.

'His name was Carl,' Lorelei went on, 'and he was really cool and nice and really quite . . . beautiful.' And then out came the story: Gina listened to every word of it, fascinated. She would replay it over and over in her mind for weeks to come.

Spring term 1980 and sixteen-year-old Lorelei was

supposed to be studying hard for her O-levels; instead she'd been falling madly in love with 'cool and nice and really quite beautiful' Carl, who was seventeen.

'He was there for me,' Lorelei told her daughter again, 'when I needed someone. I could talk and talk and talk to him. I spent all my free time with him, and all the time I wasn't with him, I was wishing I could be!'

Then the unthinkable had happened: Carl's father got a new job in London and the family had to move away in less than two months' time.

'I know this sounds crazy, Gina' – Lorelei was almost laughing at herself – 'because we weren't much older than you . . . God! We weren't much older than you at all. But we just couldn't handle the thought of being apart. We were so *obsessed* with each other – it says a lot about what else was going on in our lives, doesn't it? That we just couldn't face being separated.'

Then there was a pause, but Gina waited, hoping that the rest would come.

'We made a plan to run away together.' Lorelei's voice was low. 'He had a motorbike and a tent, and we were planning to go to France. I think we were going to pick fruit . . . or grapes, or wash dishes or something. It was so romantic and so totally nuts!' she added quickly.

'Anyway, I had packed a rucksack and we were going to leave in the middle of the night. I don't know why we had to leave at night – maybe because we were spending so much time reading Beat poetry or something . . . So . . .'

Then came a pause and a trembling sigh, which made Gina grip the phone tightly.

'But he crashed his bike,' Lorelei said. 'Well . . . some idiot driver didn't see him at a junction, pulled out and went straight into him.'

'Oh no!' Gina cried, feeling a lump in her throat.

'Oh, honey, he wasn't killed,' Lorelei went on, 'but he was a mess. He broke a wrist, his legs had to be pinned, his face needed fifty-eight stitches; it was seven months before he could walk properly again . . . and . . . well, when his parents found out the full story, they were absolutely furious. I was allowed to visit him in hospital once and that was it. They froze me – and my newly bleached blonde hair, by the way – totally out and I was devastated.

'So . . . no big surprise that the subjects you really have to study for: chemistry and *history* – there was enough emphasis on that for Gina to suspect that her mom remembered Miss Ballantyne very well – 'I flunked . . . But they let me back for my A-levels . . . so I'm very grateful to St Jude's really.'

'You should have told me all this,' Gina said.

'Should I?'

'Yes!'

'I think I was going to,' her mom began. 'I think I was waiting until you were old enough to really understand. And I guess you are now . . . First love, baby – it's just incredible and I hope you enjoy every moment of it, but it always seems to end with broken glass of one kind or another.'

'Did he move to London?' Gina wanted to know.

'Yeah . . . He sent me a postcard with his new address! But I never wrote back – it was all just too upsetting.'

'So you messed up your O-levels and went to a different school for a year?'

'Yeah, a college in Frankfurt, where Dad was based. He got better and then St Jude's let me back for my A-level year. Even though I was still way too into hair bleach and eyeliner!'

'And you did really well.'

'Yeah, but that doesn't mean you get to mess up your first exams!' Lorelei warned.

'Hey . . . it's OK. Looks like I might finally do better than you at something! Thanks for telling me, Mom,' Gina added, holding the receiver right up against her ear. 'All I want is for you to be honest with me.'

'Ha! Honest?' Niffy, cramming a large chunk of chocolate into her mouth and stretching her long arms out along the fire-escape railing, couldn't help laughing at this. 'Parents are never honest. I don't know why not . . . Apparently it's because they're trying to protect us from the ugly, evil, bitter truth.'

'Yeah, but we usually find out about it anyway and then they just look really stupid,' Amy added, a significant memory of her own popping to mind. In the holidays she'd walked in on her dad's 'business meeting' in the hotel in Dubai. '*Oh, that kind of business,*' she'd managed to say to the bare behind in front of her, before backing out of the room and slamming the door shut.

'Why didn't you just tell me?' she'd asked her dad in a flood of tears later in the day. 'Why should I be the last to know?'

'I didn't know what to say,' he'd insisted, fighting back tears of his own. 'I had no idea what you'd think . . . and I don't ever want you to think badly of me.'

Well, that at least had been honest.

'But now I think you're a liar as well as everything else,' Amy had told him. 'Can't you just be honest? With me as well as everyone else?'

But Amy wasn't being honest now, was she? She still hadn't mentioned one word about her father's new life to her friends. And she'd already told him that she would . . .

Min took the slab of chocolate from Niffy and broke off a piece. All four girls were out on the fire escape: it was after ten p.m., so they were confined to their dorm, but it was such an amazing evening, the sun still visible in the sky, that they couldn't bear to go to sleep yet.

'I asked my mum why she was so desperate for us all to be doctors,' Min told them, 'and do you know what she said? It totally surprised me – I'd thought it was because she wanted us all to have great jobs and earn good money so that she could be proud of us all – but she told me it was because she and my father still feel guilty that they had such a good education and can afford to give us one too.

'The only way of getting over the guilt is for us to

work helping people less fortunate than us. If she'd told me that before, I think I'd have understood it. Instead I just felt this terrible pressure that I couldn't veer from their course.'

'What about my mum?' Niffy added. 'She's the biggest liar of them all. Apparently she didn't want me to worry . . . she still doesn't want me to worry. She wants me to stay on here and pretend that everything is just fine!'

'You must be so scared,' Gina said, rubbing Niffy's shoulder.

'I'm not as scared as I was when I first found out.' Niffy broke off another chocolate chunk and thought-fully nibbled a little corner from it. 'Why do we not have fags and booze?' she asked.

'You're going to live at home,' Amy reminded her. 'You'll have to adapt your vices. Chocolate and chips from now on.'

'I'll be the size of a house the next time you see me.' Niffy held her arms out wide to demonstrate.

But the thought of her managing to alter her rangy frame to anything house-sized just made her friends laugh.

'I won't be in the hockey team next term!' she exclaimed, as if this thought had just occurred to her.

'Bum! Obviously Gina won't be here either . . . Willow, at least, will consider that a blessing. But what will you do without me?'

It was obvious that Amy and Min were suddenly too choked to answer this question.

'Speech Day tomorrow,' Niffy said brightly in an effort to cheer them up a little. 'Wait till you see me crossing the stage in one of Amy's poncy frocks. I think we should play Banshee Buzzword Bingo for money – that'll take our mind off . . . things.'

Chapter Twenty-Five

After lunch, Niffy and Gina went back to the boarding house to change. Speech Day, the final day of the school year, involved a huge gathering in the school hall for pupils, staff and all the parents of the leavers.

Every girl leaving the school that year crossed the podium in a dress of their own choosing, had a little summary of their academic and sporting achievements read out by the Banshee and received a handshake, a book and a round of applause for their efforts.

'You look really nice,' Gina assured Niffy, who actually just looked uncomfortable in the borrowed red summer dress, admittedly a little short at the waist and the hemline. Niffy put her feet into flat red pumps, bought specially for the occasion so she didn't have to wear riding boots again.

'I can't believe I'm leaving,' she confided. 'I keep

telling myself it's just for a short time – Mum will get better really soon and I'll be back ... But what if it isn't? What if this is it? I spend the next three years of school somewhere else, and Amy and Min ...' Niffy couldn't finish the sentence because her voice was breaking.

Gina went over and put an arm round her. 'Shhh,' she soothed. 'Your mum is so strong and so optimistic, I just know she's going to be OK. You'll be back; you'll be back really soon, and even if you're not, Amy and Min will be your friends for life. I totally believe that.'

'What about you?' Niffy put her hands to her eyes and rubbed briskly. 'Are you going to miss us?'

'Of course I'm going to miss you!' Gina said, without the slightest doubt. But California was calling. She wanted to wake up to blue skies and a dazzling ocean view every morning; she wanted pure, hot, un-adulterated sunshine. She wanted to drink root beer by the pool. She wanted to hang out with Mom, Menzie and Mick. She wanted to see all her old friends ... But she didn't like to think about how much she would miss the dorm girls.

'You've got to promise me that you'll stay in touch,' she insisted, 'and that you'll definitely, definitely visit.'

'In California?' This thought seemed to cheer Niffy up a little. 'Are we all allowed to come and visit you in California?'

'Of course!'

Min, Amy, Niffy and Gina sat together in the Year Four row listening to the Banshee's summary of the past year.

All four of them had pencils and little white score-cards on their knees. At the top of the cards they each had ten words: words which were a dead cert, like *achievement*, *pride*, *excellence* and *strive*; higher-scoring words such as *example* and *illustrious*; then everyone had two mad bonus words chosen at random – *tartan*, *penguin* – that kind of thing. These were a hundred points apiece.

'Have you heard about Llewellyn?' Niffy whispered at Amy, just loud enough for Penny to turn round and glare at them.

'No!' Amy shook her head. 'Please tell me Penny's been dumped?'

'Better than that!' Niffy insisted. 'He's been arrested for shoplifting!'

'Noooo!' Amy looked at Penny and smiled. 'Goes against the communist principles a bit, doesn't it?' she couldn't help asking her rival.

'Property is theft!' Penny hissed back.

'No, I think you'll find shoplifting is theft . . . Well, that's how the police will see it anyway.'

'Your father must be delighted,' Niffy added.

Penny flushed and looked away.

'When she thought she'd get her dad to meet her boyfriend, she didn't think it would be in court, did she?' Amy whispered as loudly as she could get away with.

A note was heading down the line of seated schoolgirls towards them. It had started with Willow, and as Min passed the small blue envelope to Gina, she saw with surprise the words *Gina the daffodil from California* scribbled over the front of it.

Although Gina could feel the glare of their form teacher burning into her back, she held the envelope down in her lap and opened it as quietly as she could.

She felt her heart speeding up a little, her throat drying as she considered what this little envelope could be.

Could it be . . . ?

Could it really . . . ?

Did this mean . . . ?

She carefully unfolded the single sheet of blue paper.

Although the writing was scribbly, she could just make it out: *Gina, you're not allowed to go back to California without saying goodbye. Please! Yrs Dermot.* Two big kisses had been added at the bottom, along with a mobile phone number.

'Dermot?' Amy guessed at once.

Gina's blush confirmed this.

'I knew it!' she whispered. 'He could never keep his eyes off you.'

'But I always thought he was flirting with Niffy!' Gina whispered back.

'That was just because he was so in lurve with you he could hardly even say your name!'

'And what about the girl?' Gina asked.

'What girl?' Amy replied.

'You know, the girl . . . the one he was . . . Oh!' With a rush of embarrassment, she realized it must have been her!

'You!' Amy made the connection at the same moment.

'Oh shut up!' Gina said, but her face was flushed pink and her eyes were sparkling. 'You are so embarrassing.'

Amy laughed, but Gina saw that she had taken hold of Niffy's hand. Their fingers were linked together and squeezing each other's hard. They'd been friends since they were ten; they'd always had each other at St Jude's. Gina couldn't help wondering how Amy was going to survive Penny without Niffy by her side.

'I think we can all agree' – up on stage, the Banshee was drawing to a close – 'that this has been a wonderful year. We are bursting with pride at our achievements.'

Min added two ticks to her card.

'Nothing stands in the way of our girls. They drive through every obstacle set before them like snow-ploughs cutting through the drifts.'

'Result!' Niffy circled a bonus word – *snowplough* – and punched the air. 'One hundred points! One hundred points!'

'And now I'd like to invite all the leavers to come and wait backstage so we can let them appear in turn and congratulate them on their achievements at the school.'

During the loud applause, Jenny, Niffy and Gina shuffled out of the Year Four row.

'I have to go to the loo,' Gina whispered to Niffy. 'I'll catch up with you backstage.'

'Luella Nairn-Bassett,' the Banshee began as Niffy stood and smiled at the edge of the stage.

'Oh no, she's put on her boots!' Amy hissed. 'Why has she taken off her pumps and put on her boots?'

'They look good,' Min countered. 'They're very Niffy.'

'I lend her my red Emporio Armani and she wears it with riding boots!'

'Luella is a boarder who joined us when she was ten years old.' The Banshee was smiling kindly: clearly all thoughts of finding Niffy in the herbaceous border and her shoe in the records room were far from her mind. 'She's been captain of every one of her year's lacrosse, hockey and tennis teams, so we're going to miss her sporting prowess terribly. Luella is going to be schooled closer to home for the foreseeable future due to family illness.'

She nodded and Niffy took her cue to walk across the stage while the audience clapped.

Only Min saw the silent tears dripping from the end of Amy's nose onto her long-forgotten scorecard.

'And now Gina Peterson,' the Banshee began. 'Gina?'

Chapter Twenty-Six

Gina was the last girl left in Daffodil dorm. School had closed at twelve noon, and after a sandwich lunch at the boarding house, everyone else had taken taxis to the airport or train station or been picked up by their parents.

Amy's dad – 'Head-to-toe Versace, Dad: you are so embarrassing!' 'Hey, I'm a Glasgow boy and proud of it!' – had arrived with his partner, Gary Livingstone.

'*Business* partner?' Niffy had asked Amy quietly, wanting to clarify.

'No.' Amy had played it extremely coolly. 'The other kind. Can't you tell? They're wearing the same shoes. They must have been shopping together, which is kind of sweet.'

'Very,' Niffy had agreed, taking it completely in her stride, but then she'd had to ask, 'Why do we know nothing about this? You've obviously known since . . .'

'Dubai,' Amy had told her.

'Were you worried about what we'd think?' Niffy had asked in surprise.

'No,' Amy had replied. 'I was too busy worrying what *I* thought about it.' She'd taken a deep breath, then smiled. 'And I've decided it's OK.'

'Of course it's OK! It's totally fine. Cool. Look, your dad is introducing Gary to my mum,' Niffy had observed.

Both girls had watched as Mrs N-B, whose social training had begun in toddlerhood, shook Gary's hand, then declared, 'Oh really! Lucky you! He's been on the shelf for far too long.'

'Yeah, and now we know why,' Amy had told Niffy. 'Turns out my dad is gay.'

'Did you have any idea before?' Niffy had wondered.

'You know, I think I did. I think he's the one who was really surprised by it!'

Then it had been time for Amy, Min and Gina to say goodbye to Niffy. Lots of upbeat, encouraging 'see you later' kind of words were exchanged, but when it came to the hugs, it had been impossible to ignore the choked-up throats and welling tears.

'When do I get to visit you in California?'

Niffy had asked after hugging Gina hard.

'Whenever you like!' Gina had assured her.

When Min had put her arms round Niffy, she'd said, 'You know what I told you about school being for a few years and family being for ever . . .'

She'd felt Niffy nod against her shoulder.

'I got it the wrong way round.' Min had tried very hard not to cry. 'We only get to live at home for a few years, but school friends are for ever. OK?'

'Hey, you take care . . .' Niffy had said into Amy's hair as she held her tight. 'Keep away from that stupid Hernandez geek.'

'I will – I have a plan for him. Just as soon as Mel's supplied a diagram of his willy, I'm going to photocopy it and fly-post it on the lampposts outside St Lennox.'

'That's my girl,' Niffy had told her, finally letting go.

'You'll be back?' Amy had said, and then she'd repeated it, trying not to make it sound like a question: 'You'll be back.'

'Yeah.' Niffy had wiped at her eyes, then smiled at each of them in turn. 'You'll save a space on the fire escape for me, won't you?'

At those words, everyone had struggled to keep their cheerful smiles in place.

* * *

As the Nairn-Bassett car had pulled out of the drive-way, with Niffy waving madly until she was out of sight, a small white Interflora van had parked up. The driver had got out, then taken an extravagantly large bunch of fat pink roses out of the back.

As he'd begun to walk towards the front door of the boarding house, Amy hadn't been able to resist asking, 'So who's the lucky girl then?'

When the man had glanced down at the card and read: '*Amy McCorquodale*,' she'd nearly fallen over with surprise.

'That's me!' she'd told him and he'd handed her his clipboard to sign, passed her the enormous bouquet, then headed off in his van before she'd even fumbled open the envelope to read the card.

Min and Gina were looking over her shoulder in astonishment as she'd read out, '*I've messed everything up. Is there any chance we could start over again? Jason.*'

'Oh my God!' Amy had not been able to stop herself from laughing at this. 'What is he like?!'

'He's smitten,' Min had told her.

'A confused, smitten kitten,' Gina had confirmed.

'What am I going to do now?'

'I can't wait to find out!'

* * *

Now, only Gina was left: her flight home wasn't till later. She stood by the dorm window and looked out over the school playing fields and the running track where Min had broken the school record.

Then she heard the screech of the fire-door hinge and automatically counted the twenty seconds it took before Mrs Knebworth arrived at the door.

'Hello, Gina. Not too lonely up here, I hope?' the Neb asked.

'No, no, I'm fine,' she replied.

'So . . . we all survived the summer term, despite all the usual scrapes and disagreements.'

Gina nodded slowly.

'Good. I think you really enjoyed it in the end, didn't you?'

'Oh yeah.' Gina smiled. 'Much more than I thought I would.'

'Good. We'll all miss Luella though, won't we?'

'Yes . . . but I think she'll be back soon.'

'Yes. That's the right thing to hope for.' And Mrs Knebworth gave a smile that made her face look almost kindly. Gina wished that Amy was here to see it.

'Do you want me to order you a taxi?' the Neb asked next.

'No, I'm fine. Mom said she'd sort me out with a car – whatever that means. I think it's because I moaned so much about the taxi driver who brought me here from the airport. Anyway, she said she wants me to travel back in style. I think I'm going business class.'

'Oh, nice! It's a long journey – do you want me to pack you up some food? I won't put in too much salt or garlic!'

This made them both laugh.

'You're a dreadful bunch, really,' Mrs Knebworth added.

'What are you doing for the holidays?' Gina asked her.

'Going home!' She smiled brightly. 'I have a little house in Gullane and my daughter's back from university, so she's joining me for some of the time. I like the peace and quiet out there.'

Home? Gina had never thought of Mrs Knebworth as having anywhere else to live but the boarding house. She'd certainly not known about a daughter. All she knew about her was that she was a widow – though she'd never really thought about what that meant. Suddenly she felt a wave of sympathy for the housemistress, with a daughter she was putting through university and a job she was never allowed to escape from, except in the school holidays.

When the car arrived, Gina's eyes nearly popped out of her head. It was a long, sleek black limousine. A driver in a peaked cap and gloves got out, took her luggage and loaded it effortlessly into the boot.

'So we're off to the airport, Miss Peterson?' he asked her.

'Well . . . erm . . .' Gina checked her wristwatch: there was still plenty of time. Time enough to make the little detour she'd planned. 'Can we just head into town first?' she asked.

'Anywhere you like, miss. Your wish is my command!' he answered with a smile.

In the back seat of the car, Gina opened the mini-bar and saw that it was stacked with cans of fizzy drink, bottles of water, and crisps. She set two cans of Coke out on the table, alongside two glasses, and opened some crisps.

With a thrilling mixture of terror and excitement, she re-dialled the number on her cell phone, which had been handed back to her that morning.

As the limo pulled up in the narrow cobbled street, Gina could see an astonished face looking down from the upstairs window, then a hand waving at the sight of her.

A few moments later, Dermot O'Hagan cast off his white apron and, with his dad's permission, took two hours out from his shift. He ran out of the café, taking the stairs three at a time.

Gina waited in the car, feeling her heart pound in her chest. He was lovely! And he was so into her. Wasn't he? Of course he was . . . He was rushing down a flight of stairs to get to her. She hugged herself. This was going to be wonderful . . . wasn't it?

'Oh. My. Lord!' Dermot said when the driver opened the door for him and ushered him into the back seat beside her. 'I take back everything – every single word I ever said about never going out with girls like you. Do you always come here by driver? Why did I not know this?' he went on nervously, taking a seat, running his hands over his hair and smelling just a touch too strongly of toothpaste, mouthwash, deodorant *and* shaving cream.

'I'm just an ordinary girl, Dermot,' Gina assured him as the driver got back into the front seat and started up the engine. 'Look – it's Coke and crisps all the way, not champagne and caviar.'

She poured out the drinks and they clinked glasses

as the car set off out of town towards the airport.

'I'm really glad you could come,' she said, feeling a little shy now that he was really here, nestled into the black leather seat beside her. 'I just had to share the car with someone! Isn't it great?' She used one of the little buttons to whiz the window down, then back up again.

'Well, I'm so glad to be that someone,' Dermot said, his cheeky grin in place again.

Then a heavy silence descended and Gina frantically wondered what to say next.

'Oh no, awkward silence time,' Dermot joked. 'Oh my God! Here we are: we've been thinking and thinking about this, and now we've got absolutely nothing to say. I'm sorry – do you want me to talk about the café? What's been going on there? Or shall I tell you about what happened the last time I got on a plane . . . Which is quite a funny story, but it might put you off flying and I'm not sure that's what you need right now, is it? Or should I just try and shut up and not drive you demented before we're even on the ring road? Or how about—?'

'Shh!' she interrupted him.

'See, I *am* going to drive you demented—'

'Shh!' she interrupted again. 'Dermot! Stop it! I

think you're very nice,' she added, surprising herself and blushing furiously.

'*Nice!* Oh no! No one ever tells James Bond he's "nice". I don't think it's a good sign. I really do not think this is a good sign at all,' he babbled anxiously.

'Dermot!'

Gina moved along the seat just a little so she nudged up against him. He *was* nice. He was in his blue shirt again – the one that made his blue eyes leap out at you. And she liked the fact that he was nervous and jumpy and had obviously over-prepared in the bathroom for this meeting.

'So . . . busy afternoon in the café?' she asked, because it was all she could think of, even though right now she couldn't have cared if the café was on fire.

'Oh, you know . . .'

She noticed that his arm had moved down from the top of the seat and was now round her shoulders, but she didn't mind. Not in the slightest; no, she liked it. It felt warm and heavy against her. Not even the tiniest bit tentacle-like.

He turned to look at her. 'I've been told not, under any circumstances, to kiss you,' he blurted out.

'Huh? Who told you that?'

'Your friend – the skinny one – everyone calls her

Smelly or something, but I'm hoping that's just a nickname.'

'Niffy? She told you not to kiss me?'

'Yup, she said you're allergic to kissing or something . . . which is, you know, interesting. I think.'

Gina looked closely at Dermot: he had a wide mouth and strong white teeth with a little gap between the front two. She thought that she'd never wanted to kiss anything more than she wanted to kiss Dermot's mouth.

'Will you stop talking?' she asked, although really she was interested to hear what Dermot had to say about everything: very, very interested.

'On one condition,' he said.

But she didn't wait to hear what the condition was, because she'd leaned up to meet his mouth with hers. She just knew she was ready for this. Ready to kiss Dermot, yes; but ready for so much more. She wanted to be with him, she wanted to talk to him, know what he thought about things. He wasn't just going to be a fumbly snog or an awkward experience. He was going to be her friend, her first real *boyfriend*.

Whatever Niffy had said about kissing – Gina couldn't quite remember it, because she was a little bit lost and smudgy and fuzzy about the edges right now – but whatever it was, it had been about right.

When that magical, wonderful first kiss was finally over, Dermot looked into her eyes and said, 'I am so, so sorry you're going back home. I think I'm going to cry at the airport.'

This only made her smile because, with her heart so happy at her big decision, she told him, 'It's just for the holidays. I'm coming back to St Jude's in August.'

She'd not walked out onto the stage on Speech Day. She'd decided that her English teacher, Mrs Parker, and some of the other St Jude's teachers, were going to be more useful to her than the ones at her old school. She'd decided she was going to get much, much better GCSEs than her mother – if it killed her. She'd also decided she wanted to spend a lot more time hanging out with Dermot. And most importantly of all, she'd decided that, right now, Amy and Min needed her more than Paula, Ria and Maddison did.

So yes . . . in the hope that California would always be there to go home to, she'd decided she was definitely, definitely coming back to Scotland next term for more.

Acknowledgements

There are two people without whom *Secrets at St Jude's* would never have come about: my fabulous agent, Darley Anderson and Random House Children's Books Fiction Publisher, Annie Eaton. For your many suggestions, kind encouragement and enthusiasm, I am truly grateful.

Julia Churchill at the agency has also been a star, reading early chapters and generally cheering me on! Thank you so much. To Emma, Maddie, Zoe and Ella: I hope you all know how much I appreciate your hard work on my behalf.

An enormous thank you to Kelly Hurst for being such a sensitive, thoughtful and all round brilliant editor, it's been a pleasure! Likewise, to copy-editor Sophie Nelson: many, many thanks. I am hugely grateful for the effort and enthusiasm of so many lovely RHCB people.

I have to mention my own teen gang, remembered very fondly while I was writing this: loads of love (and don't worry, names have been changed!). All my very best to John Elder – although he'll want his pupils to put this book down and go and read something much more serious instead!

Finally: TQ, I owe you, as always. S and C . . . I'm so looking forward to hearing what you think!

About the Author

Carmen Reid is the author of several bestselling adults novels. Secrets of *St Judes's: New Girl* is her first novel for young adults.

After working as a journalist in London she moved to Glasgow, Scotland, where she looks after one husband, two children, a puppy, three goldfish and writes almost all the rest of the time.

Visit her website at www.carmenreid.com